Sweet

Forgiveness

SWEET FORGIVENESS

INDIGO BAY SWEET ROMANCE SERIES

JEAN ORAM

Sweet Forgiveness

Indigo Bay Sweet Romance Series
By Jean Oram

© 2018 Jean Oram
First Edition

Printed in the United States of America unless otherwise stated on the last page of this book. Published by Oram Productions Alberta, Canada.

LIBRARY OF CONGRESS CATALOGING-IN-PUBLICATION DATA

Oram, Jean.

Sweet Forgiveness / Jean Oram.—1st. ed.

p. cm.

ISBN: 978-1-928198-56-7 (paperback) Ebook ISBN: 978-1-928198-57-4

1. Romance fiction. 2. Romance fiction—Small towns. 3. Small towns—Fiction. 4. Indigo Bay (Imaginary place)—Fiction. 5. Interpersonal relations—Fiction. 6. Indigo Bay Sweet Romance Series—Series. 7. Romance fiction, American. 10. Man-woman relationships—Fiction. 11. Romances. 12. FICTION / Romance / Contemporary. I. Title.

First Oram Productions Edition: May 2018

Cover design by Najla Qamber Designs

ACKNOWLEDGMENTS

Thank you to my Beta Sisters, Erika Howder, Lucy Jones, Donna Wolz, Sharon Sanders, Sarah Albertson, Margaret Cambridge, Connie Williams Mechling, and Debra Lee. Your help with Zoe and Ashton, as well as with the South was instrumental in making this story the best it could be.

Some of my readers are aware of the troubles I have in naming my characters. (My second born came home from the hospital with a tentative name, so apparently this 'issue' of mine doesn't remain solely with fictional characters.) With well over 100 named characters now, I'm finding the task of naming characters trickier with each book that I write. So, in this book, with Zoe having five fur babies, I decided to take the easy way out. I mean, um, grant a few of my Jeansters the honor of naming three of Zoe's feline friends! A big thanks goes to Ruth Hufford for naming the kitty character Pandora. I had written a cat into the early draft who liked boxes, and when Ruth suggested this name, I knew it was a winner. Karen McNicol named the second cat, Mishka, which got quite a few votes in my reader group. And finally we have Binx which is a totally cool sounding name which was chosen by Deborah Thompson Alderman. Thank you for all the wonderful pet names, Jeansters. I may have to ask you to name my future human characters as well!

I'd also like to thank you Margaret Carney for her wonderful editing tweaks and comments that helped putting the finishing touches on the story, and for Emily Kirkpatrick for catching any last whoopsies!

As well, thank you to my fellow Indigo Bay authors both past and present, for building this world with me. It's been a blast!

BONUS SCENES

ONE YEAR AGO—AUGUST

ZOE

Zoe Ward began packing boxes of books and journals, humming under her breath. She lifted her calico cat, Pandora, out of the box she filled with framed photos. She had a feeling she would soon be hanging them on the walls of her new home with Ashton Wallace. That was, if the way the two of them had been talking was an indication.

Today, while walking the beach after breakfast, he'd pointed to a town house that was for sale a block from the Atlantic Ocean. He'd taken a photo of the Realtor's phone number, suggesting they take a look around, since his one-year bachelor suite rental lease was coming up for renewal in a month. Maybe they could buy a place together.

She'd barely been able to breathe, she'd been so excited. Now, hours later, she was using her nervous energy for good and packing up clutter so her small house would show better should she need to put it up for sale.

Zoe abandoned the box and hummed and danced her way across her bedroom to check her cell phone. She was expecting a text from Ashton, since it was just about bedtime. Texting goodnight was part of their daily routine, and it was a ritual she looked forward to. Tonight, as per their Friday night tradition, she had made them spaghetti and meatballs from her grandmother's recipe. Then they'd walked the beach before a lingering, sweet goodnight kiss.

There was no text yet, and Zoe sent him an emoji of a happy face blowing a kiss.

The past two and a half months had been a whirlwind. She'd managed to keep a check on her usual desire to move along too quickly, but Ashton had been right there, urging them to move faster, talking about their future and creating mutual dreams for them to share. It was perfect. *He* was perfect, and she couldn't wait to make him hers.

After being left the night before her wedding thirteen years ago, she'd been waiting for a man like him. One who wouldn't claim she was smothering him, or acting too clingy. One who was as into commitment and sharing each other's lives as she was.

Zoe set down her phone and smiled as she picked up a framed photo of Ashton. She waltzed across the room with it and placed it on her newly cleared off bedside table. She pressed a kiss on her fingertips, then gently brushed the frame's glass.

There was a knock at her door and she went to answer it. Her cat Houdini was perched nearby and she scooped him up so he wouldn't escape.

She opened the door to find Ashton there. Her heart lifted, thinking he had come all the way back for one more kiss.

But there was no hug that swept her into his arms, no kiss, no upturn of his lips, even. He came in, closing the door behind him as she released her cat.

She pulled Ashton into a careful embrace. "Are you okay?"

He let out a shuddered breath, holding her tight. "I have to go to the city to take care of some personal business."

Zoe released him, letting her hands drift to his shoulders, so she could watch his expression. "I'll come with you."

"I think it would be best if I went alone."

She stepped back, wishing she still had the cat to hold. "What do you mean, alone?"

"It's a big mess I have to straighten out. You don't need to worry over it. I'll be home tomorrow night."

"You don't need to protect me from your life, Ash. Worry is what people do for their loved ones. I want to help even if it's messy." Only two weeks ago he'd been right there, holding the bucket for her when she'd had the flu. They were past the life-is-perfect stage of their relationship.

But he didn't appear convinced.

"Let me help," she insisted.

He placed a kiss on her forehead. "I don't want to get into it right now. I'll tell you all about it when I'm home again."

"Is everyone all right?"

"Yeah. I just…" He paused on his way to the door. "I need some space to figure things out."

Space.

That was never a good word.

Why had he been talking about buying a house together if he wasn't ready? Had she missed the signs again? Had she somehow been pushing him into things he didn't truly want or wasn't ready for?

"Is this about us moving in together?" she asked.

He looked surprised, then confused. "What? No. Why?"

Zoe toyed with her necklace while draping her free arm across her gut. "Oh. Um, I don't know. It just seems like we're moving really fast and suddenly you're... You know what? It's fine. I'm just worried and want to help, that's all."

"I thought you were okay with where things were moving with us."

"Yeah! No, I am fine. Great, even. Are you?"

He gave her a strange look. "Yes." He shook his head as though trying to remove the crazy vibe that had settled around them. "I'll call you."

"When?" She winced, realizing she sounded needy.

He let out a slow breath, and the pinched, pained look that was there earlier returned. "Hopefully, when I get home tomorrow night."

"Well then, until tomorrow." She opened the door for him, letting him out. "If you need anything, you know where to find me."

He turned back, looking so much like the handsome man she loved and trusted in the fading twilight that the worry she'd been feeling vanished. "Thanks. For understanding."

"I'll always be here for you."

He smiled softly, brushing her cheek with his thumb. "It's what I love best about you."

He kissed her in a lingering way that somehow felt like a goodbye, and she shivered when he left.

Whatever was happening was big, and all the more reason he should've shared it with her. But...

Space.

She truly hated that word.

ASHTON

ASHTON PARKED in front of the high-rise apartment he remembered from six months ago. It felt like it had been a lifetime, which was ironically appropriate.

Palm trees lined the front walk and the grass was green despite the pervasive Charleston heat. Before Zoe, Ashton had dated Maliki for a few months. Even from the start he'd known in his gut it wouldn't work out. And then she'd proved it by breaking up with him because he always smelled like cinnamon buns from Sweet Caroline's in Indigo Bay. She'd claimed it was making her crave sweets, causing her to gain weight.

He chuckled under his breath. What a silly reason for a break up. But those cinnamon buns had led him directly to Zoe. Indigo Bay guest Ginger McGinty had matched the two of them up based on their love of the buns.

Zoe.

He hadn't been straight with her last night and he felt conflicted. He'd wanted to protect her, not cause her unnecessary worry—especially since so much of what he knew, and thought he might do, was mere speculation. Once he talked to Maliki and had a plan, then he'd tell Zoe everything and more. They'd figure things out together.

But right now...right now the only thing he knew for sure was that he wanted to protect the perfect, untainted part of his life where Zoe resided.

His time with his ex-girlfriend felt as though it had been so long ago, so unreal. But it had suddenly become so very real.

And now he was parked in front of her building at nine o'clock on a Saturday morning, wondering how he was going to figure out his life with her and with their baby, due to be born in a few months.

Ashton let his skull fall back against the headrest and closed his eyes.

Pregnant. Six months pregnant and only telling him about it now.

He'd been dropping hints around Zoe about adopting a

baby, hoping she would be on board with starting a family even though they were both well past the average age for new parents. He'd always wanted a family. And now it looked as though that wish was about to be granted.

But not with the woman he loved.

A baby changed everything.

And yet, it might change so little. He'd seen friends make stranger things work than raising a child with an ex.

He and Zoe could take the baby during the summer holidays and weekends, as well as other holidays throughout the year when the child didn't have school, and neither did he. Maliki wouldn't have to worry about finding a babysitter and, as a schoolteacher, Ashton would have plenty of time to spend with this little one. They'd find a way to share this child and give it all the love and opportunities it deserved. He wouldn't be like his selfish father, who'd skipped town, finding the burden of loving and raising a child to be too much.

With his heart full of hope, Ashton left his car and rang the buzzer in the lobby of the Charleston high-rise. Traffic whizzed by behind him and he wondered if his ex-girlfriend would consider moving to Indigo Bay. The small town on the South Carolina ocean shore would be the perfect place to raise a child, surely better than a city with traffic zipping by at all hours of the day.

He was let into the building and took the elevator to Maliki's floor.

"Hi," she said, as he approached. She'd been waiting, her apartment door open as she peeked out into the hall, watching for him.

"Hi, Maliki. You look well." He felt like a liar, but didn't know what else to say. Her pregnancy seemed to be taking a severe toll on her and she lacked an expected third-trimester glow.

"How are you feeling?" he asked.

She let him into her apartment. "Can I get you a cup of coffee?"

"I'm fine, thanks. I got some at the gas station."

"Fabulous coffee, I'm sure," she teased.

"I'm curious," he said, not bothering to beat around the bush, "why you waited so long to tell me about the baby."

Her smile faltered and she moved farther into the apartment, which had seemed fine for a single woman in her early thirties a few months ago. Now it seemed tired, worn and dark.

There was a large box for a baby crib sitting beside the faded armchair she was easing herself into.

"Do you want me to put this together?" Ashton offered, pulling the box closer, happy to have something to do with his hands.

"If you don't mind." Maliki winced as she sat.

"Are you okay?" He gazed at her. She was biting her upper lip, fighting tears.

Ashton's heart raced. "What's wrong?"

"The baby's not well."

"What?" He barely had the breath to talk. Why had she called him here—just to cruelly tell him he wasn't going to be a father?

"They're planning an early C-section. The baby will need surgery immediately after delivery." She was rubbing slow circles on her stretched stomach, as though soothing the child.

Ashton paced, feeling as though every hope he'd built up on the way over was being dashed to the ground, then stomped upon. "You're due in October? November?"

"The baby can't wait that long. They're going to induce me early."

A premature infant that needed immediate surgery. The child was going to require a lot of medical attention.

"Do you have medical insurance?"

Maliki slowly shook her head.

"Mine might cover some things. Especially for the baby. Do you know if it's a boy or a girl?"

She smiled weakly. "It's a girl. Well, they're not a hundred percent sure, but they haven't seen anything in the ultrasounds to indicate it's a boy."

"A girl." A daughter.

He already knew he'd do everything for her. Everything and anything.

He looked around the one-bedroom apartment. It needed fresh paint, new flooring, a deep cleaning. And definitely more baby stuff.

"I'll call my medical plan on Monday and see what they'll cover. Maybe not the birth, but surgery, because she'll be my dependent."

Wow, that felt real. A dependent. Someone depending on him. Depending upon him for her very life.

He stiffened as a realization struck, and he turned to his ex-girlfriend. "Is that why you called me? For medical coverage?"

Her eyes filled with tears as she looked away, and Ashton clamped down on his anger.

The child mattered more than Maliki's motivations. The baby was his, and he had rights.

Still, anger ripped through him over being so blatantly used. Ashton rubbed his forehead as he focused on keeping his emotions in check.

"You're mad," she stated.

"Of course I am!" he exclaimed. "If the baby wasn't sick would you ever have told me I was going to be a father?"

"I picked up the phone to call you so many times, but I

thought you'd be angry and I wasn't ready to face that. My whole life has changed."

Changed because of him. But she wasn't the only one with a life change.

"I'm upset because you kept this from me," he said. "There might have been something I could have helped with sooner."

"There wasn't." She stared him straight in the eye. "I promise. I'm sorry I didn't bring you in sooner. I've been dealing with things and I just…"

That was a poor excuse and they both knew it.

Ashton headed for the door. "I'll let you know if my plan will cover the baby's surgery. I expect to get custody during all holidays and weekends, if not more."

"Ashton."

The plea in her voice made him pause as he opened the door to leave. He found that she'd followed him, her face more pale than ever.

"You should rest."

"I know." Her eyelids drifted shut as she inhaled, as though bracing herself. "Our baby isn't doing well because I have a rare disorder—it's not genetic." She looked at her hands, her face a mask of grief as she said, "I'm sick, Ashton. You'll be getting full custody."

One look at her complexion and Ashton didn't have to ask why.

ZOE

ZOE RAN toward her ringing cell phone. She stubbed her toe on a box full of books, and clutched it while hopping toward her bed, falling onto the mattress as she grabbed for her phone before it went to voice mail.

It was Ashton. At long last. He'd sent a text on Saturday night saying he wouldn't be back until Sunday.

It was Sunday night.

"Are you home? How did it go?"

There was silence on the other end of the line.

"Ash?" Zoe had ordered pizza as per their Sunday night pizza-and-movie tradition, and since she hadn't heard from him, she expected him to pop over at their usual time, which was in approximately ten minutes.

"I'm sorry, I need to stay a little longer."

"In Charleston? Are things okay?"

"Things are more complicated than I'd expected," he said carefully, his voice strained.

"What do you mean?"

"I'm still figuring it out."

"Do you want to talk it through with someone?"

"I'm tired."

They were silent for a moment.

"I bumped into the Realtor at Sweet Caroline's," Zoe offered. "She says the town house's price is likely to drop soon."

"I can't afford a house right now." Ashton's tone was sharp.

Zoe opened her mouth, but couldn't think what to say, taken so off guard by his tone.

Something was definitely wrong, and her inner fears were screaming that it was her. It was like she'd taken him scuba diving, but hadn't allowed him enough time to regulate his air pressure before they rapidly descended into the watery depths. They'd gone too deep, too quickly, and he was struggling.

"If things are moving too fast…"

The doorbell rang and she went to answer it, Houdini hot on her tail.

"Things are crazy here," Ashton said, "and I'm tired and I need to get my head on straight. I didn't mean to snap. I'll talk to you in a day or two, all right?"

"When will you be home?"

"I don't know. Just...carry on without me." He ended the call.

Carry on without him?

Zoe was standing in the entry of her home, staring at her silent phone. What was happening?

The Ashton she'd just talked to wasn't the one she knew, and a part of her wanted to drive to the city, track him down and demand a proper answer. The wiser part of her told her to be patient and give him space.

The doorbell rang again and she jumped.

"Hey, Zoe."

"Hey." She paid Trenton, the usual Sunday night deliveryman, for the pizza.

"Ashton here?"

She shook her head.

"You break up?"

She looked up from the warm box he'd transferred into her hands. The bottom was already damp from the pizza's heat. "No, why?"

The man shrugged. "He's always here Sunday night." He stepped off the porch. "Tell him I owe him five bucks—that trick on helping Tyson sound out words worked wonders."

"Okay. I'll tell him."

She closed the door and shoved the pizza into the fridge without taking a slice.

What was she going to do about Ashton? Before she launched into ways to meddle in his life, she reminded herself to chill out, relax, have some faith. Guys didn't like to be pushed to talk about their feelings. Even if Ashton seemed to be different, at their root, men were men; if you pushed and pried they withdrew. And Ashton was doing that. He was shutting her out, which meant she had to tread carefully or she'd push him away even further—like she had with her ex-fiancé, who'd left her minutes after their rehearsal supper, thanks to her insistence that he resolve the stressful, ongoing fight between him and his younger brother. It had been creating tension during the party and she'd begged him to do something. He had. He'd dumped her.

And her high school sweetheart? Well, when they'd started talking about their futures he'd begun to withdraw, finally snapping at her that he was too young to be pressured into marriage. He'd left town the next day.

Ashton's behavior was unexpected, and she longed to help shoulder whatever was burdening him. But she'd also learned the hard way that the only way to keep Ashton was to fight her instincts and butt out.

ASHTON

ASHTON PACED the small apartment in Charleston. He'd slept on Maliki's couch for the past few days, and now he moved like a caged animal, eager to be set free. The room was cramped, the air conditioning barely strong enough to take the edge off the cloying city heat. It was too dark, too…too… He felt trapped.

He longed for Indigo Bay. For his own apartment. For Zoe.

The longer he was here, the less real their idealistic, easy relationship felt.

He loved her. He knew that. He knew it was real.

But it no longer seemed like it was even possible. Their relationship felt too simple in the face of everything he'd gone through here in the city over the past few days. And

Zoe, the most patient woman he knew, was starting to lose it over the phone. Instead of encouraging him to talk—which he wasn't quite ready to do, for fear of hurting her somehow with the mess of thoughts running through his head, or worse, have her convince him to give in to his secret wishes and to walk away from the baby and all it's upcoming needs —she'd begun to go silent.

Zoe. Silent.

She wasn't encouraging him to express his fleeting thoughts, wasn't helping him find the right path, like she had over whether to pursue a master's degree, or over which car to lease.

She seemed almost indifferent. As though she'd put up a wall to keep him out.

Their relationship wasn't strong enough for this, and she didn't deserve a mess, or a man who would be splitting his attention for the next year or even longer.

Maliki came home from her waitressing job, entering the apartment with slow steps. He worried once again what impact her physical issues might be having on the baby. She needed to take time off, rest more, but she couldn't afford to.

To prevent her from overdoing it, Ashton had been encouraging her to put her feet up in the evenings while he did the shopping, cooking and cleaning. He feared he would soon resent spending his summer vacation helping Maliki, as he wished he was with Zoe, helping her, having a baby with her.

"Hi," Maliki said, dropping her purse on a chair at the kitchen table.

"Are you thirsty? Can I get you some water?" Ashton offered.

She looked lifeless, her skin drained of vitality. Since her pregnancy, she'd had to go off some of her illness-regulating medications, and the effect, compared to a few months ago, was astounding. Back then he hadn't even been aware she had health issues.

"I've been peeing every half hour. Everything I drink goes right through me." She smiled, not put off by his nagging. "Thank you for doing laundry." She rested a hand on a stack of fluffy towels, still warm from the dryer that was located a few floors above the apartment.

"I wished you'd called me sooner so I could help out more."

"It wouldn't change anything. I was doing fine until a few weeks ago."

Ashton chewed on his bottom lip, hands on his hips. He couldn't imagine what would happen if he went back to Indigo Bay. The very idea felt like a death sentence to their unborn child.

He shuddered at the thought. Maliki and the baby needed help. Unfortunately, neither he nor Maliki could afford to hire someone. It was fine now, as he had summer holidays, but in less than a month he'd be back at work and there'd be nobody to care for her. With them unwed, he couldn't even take a paid leave to stay with her.

"Did you add any names to the baby list?" she asked, sitting at the kitchen table. She glanced up at the notepaper stuck to the fridge. "I hope you didn't cross off Sophie. I love that name."

"I didn't even think about names today." Whenever he tried, he simply wasn't able to think, hope or dream about their unborn child. "I heard back from the insurance company." He'd been hounding them for an answer for days.

"What did they say?" she asked, hope lighting her expression.

"They won't cover you because of the preexisting medical condition, but they'll cover most of the birth, since a C-section is for the baby's well-being, and she's my dependent. They'll also cover 80 percent of her surgeries."

"Oh, thank goodness." Maliki let out a long breath of relief.

Ashton had to sit down and draw a deep breath. It felt awful to be talking about money and insurance coverage when two lives were hanging in the balance.

Early in Maliki's pregnancy she'd been presented with the choice of either terminating it and saving her own life by continuing her medications—which weren't safe for the baby —or stopping them and continuing with her pregnancy. She'd chosen the baby's life over her own, even knowing that nine months without medication made it unlikely she'd survive beyond the baby's first year.

The fact that she'd had to make that choice and had chosen their child left Ashton shaking with emotion. It was unfair. Unjust. And there was nothing he could do but be there for the two of them, try to keep things together, and give the baby and her mother the best possible chance.

"Supper's in the slow cooker," he said, feeling the need for air, space, anything but be here where impending death and sadness lingered like an unwanted guest. "It'll be ready at five thirty. I need to run out and pick up some lettuce."

"Thank you," Maliki said, reaching over to rest a cool hand on his. "For everything."

"I'm sorry there isn't more I can do."

"You're a good man. You've already done so much for us."

He was unable to speak, stuck to the spot on the old, worn floor. He'd offered so little compared to her sacrifices. He couldn't imagine making such an impossible choice like she had. She'd given up everything for their daughter, for him. She would barely get to know her own child, and surely wouldn't be remembered.

She'd given so much, and he was going to walk away with a precious, wonderful child.

Maliki reached up to wipe the wetness from his cheeks with a sad smile. "It's all going to work out as it's supposed to."

He stood, a sudden strength of conviction running through him. "Marry me."

She gave a start. "What?" she asked softly.

"It makes perfect sense."

"We don't love each other."

"That doesn't matter. I could take a paid leave to care for you. My medical plan would cover things neither of us can afford such as your obstetrician appointments. Now until you have the baby. And then medical needs afterward, too." There would certainly be a lot of those for both the baby and Maliki, and financially it was more than he could bear.

"That's insurance fraud."

"We're having a baby together, Maliki. Who's going to question marriage?"

Zoe would. Otherwise, nobody.

"My conditions are pre-existing."

"I know, but being married will help with other things, too." As her husband, he'd have more rights and be able to help more.

Maliki inhaled sharply as she comprehended that he was referring to end-of-life scenarios where as her husband he could avoid legal battles and permissions to take care of things. She rested the tips of her fingers on the end of her nose as tears filled her eyes. She nodded.

He swallowed hard, hating himself for bringing up her mortality—the one thing she must be trying to outrun.

"Forget I said anything," he said.

"No." She began crying. "You're right. And I don't want this baby to feel like I did, growing up. I want her to feel like she had a family, that she didn't have one more mark against her because her mom and dad weren't married and never lived together. I want her to think she was loved. That her life was normal and perfect before her mother...before I..."

"She *will* be loved. Her life will be incredible."

Maliki sobbed, falling against his shoulder, wetting it with her tears.

"Everything will go to you," she said quickly. "There'll be no dispute over custody. Nobody will fight you, and you can give her the life she deserves." She grabbed his shirt, her expression pleading. "Please, Ashton. Promise me that."

"There won't be a fight. I'm her father."

This was the right thing to do. The right thing to do for the mother of their child. The right thing for their daughter.

"We can do this, Maliki. For our baby girl."

She leaned against him even harder. "Thank you."

"Consider it done." And as Ashton helped her to bed so she could rest, he tried hard not to think of the woman he truly wanted, the one who had captured his heart back in Indigo Bay.

ZOE

ZOE HADN'T SEEN Ashton since last Friday night and had barely slept a wink since then.

Something had changed. He'd called her from the city hours ago, asking to talk at long last, and she'd been pacing her small home as she waited into the late hours of the night for his arrival.

When his car's headlights finally appeared and he parked on the street, she went to the door, wondering where they would be next spring. Before talk of buying a house together, he'd promised to landscape her yard. The bushes around the place needed care and attention, and he'd planned a gazebo in the back so she could read in the shade on the weekends while sipping cold drinks.

But that promise had fallen to the wayside, replaced by something even better. But as Ashton turned off his car, she shivered, knowing instinctively what was coming. Despite saying he wanted to talk, he'd withdrawn, holding back pieces of his life, no longer letting her in.

He was going to ask for more space. He was going to break up with her.

Ashton got out of his car, his movements so unlike those she recognized that for a moment she thought it was someone else. He looked as though the weight of the world was dragging him under, as though he was pulling a boat ashore, back bent, each step an effort as he came up the walkway.

"Want to come in?" she asked.

With one hand clutching the thin metal railing, he paused.

"Ash?" she said, when he didn't reply. Finally he looked up, his expression etched in pain.

She flew down the steps, halting in front of him, stopping herself from reaching out when he shook his head.

"I'm sorry."

"Where have you been?" she asked. "Is everything okay? I've been so worried." She backed up a step, then another one. "You look like you could use a seat. And maybe a stiff drink."

Maybe he wasn't here to ask for space. Maybe something tragic had happened.

He didn't follow her, and she stood halfway up the porch steps, uncertain where to go, what to do, what to say.

"I have to leave Indigo Bay."

"Is everything okay?"

A cool breeze blew up the street from the ocean and she wrapped her arms around herself to ward off the chill.

"I know this seems sudden," he said, his voice hollow.

"Will I see you on weekends? Holidays?"

"I'm going to be busy with some things. I think it's best we break up."

Zoe couldn't breathe. Couldn't make her body do anything.

Was this what shock felt like? She'd known she was losing him, had known what was going to happen tonight, but somehow it still felt unexpected.

She hadn't pushed him, hadn't forced him to open up. It made no sense. None at all.

"Why?" The pain in her own voice made her sit heavily on the step.

His expression was blank, weary.

She struggled to make her mouth work, to ask what had happened in Charleston, what had changed everything so suddenly, so severely. He used to talk to her. They had something special. She couldn't have imagined it all.

"Ash? Please. Talk to me. I *love* you."

"I can't. I'm sorry." He was backing away, close to fleeing as she could sense he wanted, needed to. When he looked up, it was with such pain it choked her. "Zoe, I'm getting married."

CHAPTER 1

How many cats make you a cat lady?

Zoe Ward looked at the question she'd typed into the search bar of her work computer's browser, then slowly backspaced over it with a sigh.

As the owner of five cats, she was fairly certain she was already more than halfway there. But at least her rescued felines hadn't claimed she was moving too fast when she'd fallen for them. Not that her ex-boyfriend, Ashton Wallace, had actually said that. But enough men in the past had, so she'd understood the signs when he'd suddenly withdrawn despite the way he'd been talking about them moving in together.

Why was she even thinking of Ashton? It had been almost a year, and quite frankly she should be over him. She needed to go find someone nice, get married, adopt some kids, since she was probably too old to have her own now, and call it done. The problem was, she'd truly believed Ashton was the real deal, and now nobody seemed to measure up.

"There's my favorite employee!" called a deep voice.

Zoe swiveled in her office chair, spied her boss

approaching and wondered how long she'd been staring at her computer, off task and in plain sight of anyone moving through the resort's lobby. Dallas Harper, the resort owner, leaned against one of the marble columns Zoe's guest services desk was set between. He was in his mid-thirties, trim, tall and, as always while at work, sporting a peacock-blue polo shirt with the resort's logo on the breast pocket.

"Not taking a coffee break?" he asked. "Is this because of the stunned bird that little girl brought in earlier? I can watch it for you." He leaned over her desk to check for the box containing the ruby-throated hummingbird that had flown into one of the building's glass doors earlier, distressing their young guest. Since then, Zoe had cut out a dozen bird silhouettes and taped them to the windows and glass doors of the main building to act as a bird deterrent.

"I released it back into the South Carolina wilds about thirty minutes ago," Zoe said, clutching her insulated cup of sweet tea. Technically, it was indeed time for her afternoon break, but she generally took it at her desk these days due to the pathetic fact that she couldn't face the cinnamon buns from Sweet Caroline's, which more often than not arrived in the break room by three. Dallas's mother, the owner of the café, baked a large batch for resort guests, and any leftovers went to staff. The buns were like tasting heaven itself, and it had been Zoe and Ashton's mutual love of the dessert that had led a matchmaking guest, Ginger, to set them up on their first date. Seeing those sticky, yummy buns each afternoon—something she used to share with Ashton during her breaks—reminded her how naive and oblivious she'd been. She'd believed that he'd been keeping pace, and that everything was fine. Perfect even, when he'd started contacting Realtors to find them a place to share.

Obviously, everything had not been fine. He'd gone away one weekend to take care of something in the city, and had returned seven days later to break up with her. A week after that he'd married someone else.

Zoe slammed her cup down a little too hard onto the desk's granite surface.

"Are you okay?" Dallas asked gently.

"Sorry, did you need something?" Zoe asked, taking a soothing breath and ignoring his familiar, concerned look. He knew Ashton was a taboo subject, especially after he'd spent weeks following the August breakup insisting that there had to be more to the story, since she claimed she'd scared him straight into marrying someone else. Which, of course, Dallas took as evidence to support his case that there *was* more to the story.

Zoe crossed her arms, wishing away the familiar stab of betrayal that hit her square in the heart whenever she thought of Ashton and how quickly he'd moved on.

She was happy now, right? She got to do things such as organize weddings at the resort, and ensure couples didn't have to deal with the pressure of last-minute details, which could lead to breakups. She helped others reach their happily ever afters.

Sure, she was a bit lonely at times, but at least Ashton hadn't waited until their wedding rehearsal dinner to dump her, like her ex-fiancé, Kurtis, had over a decade ago. That had been a truly heart-numbing experience.

It would have been unnecessarily complicated if Ashton had left her after they'd moved in together. Really, the breakup had been a blessing in disguise.

But she still did half-wonder if Dallas was correct about there being more to the story...

Zoe took a plate of coconut-and-chocolate cookies—haystacks—from her desk drawer. "I baked something for you."

"Are you looking for a raise?" Dallas said with a chuckle.

He'd already snatched the plate from her, peeled back the wrap and was sinking his teeth into one of the small clusters. His eyes rolled, the stress that had been etched in the lines of his face softened. His moan of happiness warmed her insides.

She smiled. "Just saying thanks. Again."

"I couldn't leave you homeless," he said around a morsel. "Not for my favorite employee."

Two weeks ago a broken pipe had flooded her small house while she was at work. She'd come home to find a foot of water in the house and seven yowling kitties perched atop cupboards and bookshelves. Her collection of signed science fiction books had been ruined, and it had taken Mishka, a Persian, a week to forgive her for the injustice of not only being flooded out, but for having to move to a new home, too. The feline, however, hadn't minded Zoe handing off the two playful orange tabbies she'd been fostering to another rescue volunteer.

Luckily, Dallas had allowed her and her five remaining felines to stay in one of the resort's oceanside cottages while insurance fixed the mess. The deal was she had a free place to stay as long as she didn't go over his five-cat limit, and that she'd do a deep cleaning when she moved out. Plus if a long-term reservation came their way, she'd be out with barely a moment's notice.

"Totally my favorite," Dallas said again.

"What are you up to, Dallas Harper?" She knew from experience that when he called her his favorite employee it typically meant he had a project for her—such as organizing a wedding—or bad news.

"Nothing. We should probably talk about your cottage, though…"

A spike of worry flashed through Zoe. The unit was an older one, at the back of the resort. It was rarely booked unless there was a conference or large wedding. And right now, even though a small conference was taking place, nobody had needed the cottage—she'd checked that morning, like she always did when she arrived at her desk, and again before she left it at the end of the day. Was the cottage up for more renovations?

"Before we get into that," Dallas said, helping himself to a second haystack, "I have a little project I'm hoping you can help with. A newsletter."

That didn't seem big enough to explain the way he'd suddenly begun avoiding eye contact. Nope. There was definitely something else going on, and she had a feeling whatever it was would leave her without a place to live.

"Do I need to move?" Zoe asked Dallas, just as a tall man came up to her desk. She turned to him with a smile, frustrated by his timing. "Hello, may I help you?"

The man had a long, faint scar running down his cheek, but a friendly smile. "Has Quentin Valant checked in?" he asked.

Zoe considered sending him to Margie at the reservation desk, but with Dallas right beside her, she quickly brought up the list of bookings, tempted to skip over to her cottage's to see if anything had popped up over the past few hours. "Sorry, I don't see a reservation under that name. When are you expecting him?"

"I'm not sure. Maybe I'll check again tomorrow." The man crossed the lobby and headed back into the heat of the bright June sun.

Dallas brushed chocolate crumbs from around his mouth. "You know you could have sent him to Margie at the main desk."

"Your favorite employee wouldn't have shuffled a potential guest off like that."

He chuckled and asked, "So what do you think? A resort

newsletter that can be emailed here and there? It's long overdue."

It was a good idea. They could remind past guests of all they offered—deals, retreats, honeymoons, the works. Maybe even a behind-the-scenes or employee feature to make the place feel like home rather than some faceless corporation.

"I'm on it. When do you want the first one to go out?" Zoe turned back to her computer and brought up her browser, glad she'd removed her earlier cat lady search query, and typed in "How do you start a newsletter?"

Dallas came around her desk to peer over her shoulder. "Do you know how to do this?"

"Nope. But I will by tomorrow."

"That's why you're my favorite."

Her smile faltered as she scanned the search results. Wow. There was a pile of information, warnings, tips and legalities. She had no clue what DKIM, sequencing or double opt-in meant. She didn't even know which software program to sign up for.

"Looks like a headache," Dallas said, slowly backing away.

"Are you sure I should be doing this? Maybe the guy who does our website should take care of it."

"Ethan Mattson? He doesn't do newsletters. I already asked. But I leave it in your capable hands to learn and achieve, or whatever else you usually say about projects like this."

Zoe leaned back in her chair. "I'm not sure my hands are capable in this regard."

"Take all the time you need."

She sighed. Dallas knew she'd take on this project, just like she did anything he sent her way.

He was already starting to sneak off, the plate of treats in hand.

"Hey!" she called after him. "What were you going to say about the cottage?"

Dallas stopped and glanced back at her, but his eyes darted to the right like they did whenever he had something he didn't want to tell her.

"There's a reservation on it, isn't there?"

Zoe caught movement outside the foyer's glass doors—a flock of gulls lifting into the air. She'd almost returned her attention to Dallas when the man who'd scattered the birds came into view. It was someone tall, handsome and very familiar.

Ashton Wallace. The most recent man to break her heart.

* * *

ASHTON LET the breeze off the Atlantic Ocean wash over him. Was he really here, back in Indigo Bay? Was he really going to try and make amends with Zoe after walking out on her ten long months ago?

His life had turned into such a mess since then, and he felt as though he'd been put through the emotional wringer, then right back through it again to ensure he'd been entirely flattened.

He'd trusted someone when he shouldn't have. He'd done the right thing, been a nice guy, and been used and abused as a result. He'd lost everything, including Zoe, the only woman who'd ever made him feel truly loved.

He was the poster child for a man with complicated regrets, but he was determined not to add another one to the list. He was going to ensure he did everything he could to try and patch things up.

Inhaling deeply, he moved toward the main building which housed the lobby and a few meeting spaces and ballrooms, disturbing a flock of gulls clustered on the sandy sidewalk, hoping for a handout. As Ashton reached for the lobby door he nearly turned around again. It was three in the afternoon, time for Zoe's coffee break, and the box in his hand he'd picked up at Sweet Caroline's was emitting a delicious scent that took him back to happier times.

Weekday coffee breaks with Zoe. Conversations punctuated by laughter and kisses.

Could he face her judgment? Not only for walking out, but for returning unannounced?

What if he was about to make things worse for her by showing up? What if he was about to reopen an old wound? But just because he hadn't recovered from his didn't mean she wasn't fine and dandy without him.

He was being selfish. He was the one who wanted closure, no matter the consequences. It was him who wanted to escape the pain he'd endured in the city. Him who wanted to reclaim his cozy, wonderful life with Zoe.

She deserved more than a man like him. But she also deserved an apology and a possible reconciliation.

And if he didn't walk through those doors right now, he knew he never would, and that he would regret it for the rest of his life.

His mind made up, Ashton moved swiftly.

The foyer of the resort was quiet, a midafternoon lull that Zoe used to enjoy, as it meant she could breeze through her to-do list with few interruptions. Last summer, with his time off from teaching at the elementary school, he'd come by daily with a fresh cinnamon bun from Caroline's and join Zoe during her coffee break. Then he'd show up again at quitting time to walk her home, and sometimes he'd make her supper, sometimes she'd cook. Friday was always spaghetti at her place amid the cats, Tuesday something he'd create, and Sunday pizza and a movie on her couch.

They'd fallen into a nice rhythm. Domestic. Most men

would balk or get antsy, but Ashton had enjoyed their pattern and the feeling that he belonged. He'd been a latchkey kid, his dad a deadbeat, his mother an overworked single mom. Ashton would come home after school and watch TV alone, eat alone, do his homework alone, go to bed alone. Being with Zoe had filled that still-empty space inside him.

Each day when he'd arrive at her desk to share a cinnamon bun during her break, her face would light up, and his heart would lift in a silent reply.

Zoe had been his everything and he'd been a fool.

Today, his gaze automatically zipped toward the tall columns where her desk sat, just past the potted palms. Through the screen of leafy fronds his eyes met hers and his heart nearly stopped.

She was so beautiful.

And she was staring at him as though at a ghost.

Was she angry? Happy? He couldn't tell anything beyond her obvious shock.

Her boss, Dallas Harper, was standing by her desk, and he'd turned to see what she was gaping at.

Ashton had stopped moving, and a family of five jostled their way around him. With effort, he dragged his gaze away from Zoe to the infant in the father's arms, the spacious foyer suddenly feeling claustrophobic.

He shouldn't have blasted into Zoe's workplace as if he had the right to intrude upon her day, like old times.

He swallowed hard and came to a stop in front of her desk, unaware that he'd been propelling himself forward. "Hi."

Her expression closed as the shock wore off, and Ashton had a feeling that if it was forgiveness he was seeking, he was going to need every hour of his summer's vacation time to try and obtain even a fraction of it.

"May I help you?" Zoe's voice was tight and cold.

"Ashton, maybe I can help you at the main desk," Dallas said smoothly, hand extended to guide him away. He looked nervous, no doubt having heard the awful breakup story from Zoe's perspective and rightly siding with her.

As well, being the resort owner who'd rented Ashton a cottage for several weeks, he was also likely hoping to avoid a scene.

Ashton could see now that he should have stayed somewhere else, should have given Zoe more space. But it was hard to try and patch things up from afar. Plus nowhere else local could give him an affordable, long-term booking.

"I'm sorry, Zoe." Ashton placed the box on her desk.

"I don't want your cinnamon bun," she said tightly. When he didn't retrieve the peace offering, she picked it up, turned in her chair and dropped it into the trash. "You can't just walk in here and act like nothing has changed." Her voice had raised, carrying through the open space and drawing the attention of staff and guests. She lowered it again before adding, "That you didn't walk out of here and marry someone else."

Dallas shot him a look as if to say *Tough lucky, buddy, but she's got a point.*

Ashton focused on Zoe, not their audience. "I'll be staying in a cottage here at the resort for a few weeks, and I wanted to give you a heads-up so you weren't taken off guard."

"Enjoy your stay. And your wife."

Ashton felt the blow in his gut.

"The reservations desk can serve you." She sat up straight in her chair, rolling it closer to her computer's monitor. She said to Dallas, as though Ashton was no longer present, "I think it would be best if you sent me off to take a class on starting newsletters."

She was shutting Ashton out. As well as trying to find a way to leave town.

Not quite as bad as he'd predicted, believe it or not.

"I'm not sending you away," Dallas replied, and Ashton let out an internal sigh of relief. "We're heading into peak wedding season."

"And you now have the multi-talented Hope Ryan helping out with those. I can leave."

Zoe tucked her hair behind her ears with an earnest diligence. When she wanted something, she went for it and made it happen. Ashton's best guess was that, given her way, she'd be out of town by nightfall.

"You know I don't expect you to create a whole new career around organizing these weddings," Dallas said. "Same with the newsletter. Just throw something together."

"I haven't made weddings a full career, and you've trained us not to just 'throw things together' here at Indigo Bay Cottages."

"Giving the couple a list of local florists and caterers is sufficient."

"The brides deserve a perfect day with absolutely no hiccups that could derail things. Same with this newsletter. You want it done right. That's why you've asked me."

"They're just emails," Dallas said uncomfortably. "You write them all the time."

"Not like this. It says here there are spam laws that prohibit—"

"I know how to do newsletters," Ashton said without thinking, his mind still buzzing with the pain of Zoe's complete shutout.

The two turned to stare at him, Dallas with interest, Zoe with loathing.

"I worked on the school's in Charleston last term. I would be happy to help."

"I'm fine," she said coolly.

"I'll give you a discount on your cottage if you do," Dallas stated. He turned to Zoe. "Pull up his reservation and apply a discount code of 15 percent, please."

Zoe began typing and clicking, bringing up the guest list. Her mouth dropped open and she glared first at Dallas, then at Ashton. She was so indignant it almost looked as though she was going to cry.

Dallas immediately began apologizing to her.

"You put him in my cottage?" she said, pushing her chair back.

"I can stay in a different one," Ashton said quickly, unsure of what was going on.

"We're completely booked up," Dallas said calmly. "It's the only one I could give him long-term," he said to Zoe. "I'm sorry, but you know our deal. I was going to tell you—"

"It's fine!" Her spine straightened with an alarming ferocity as she stood, her cheeks a bright red.

She glared at Ashton. "Your cottage will be ready in an hour."

As she stormed off, she sent Dallas a parting glare, as well.

Ashton wasn't sure if the fact that she was talking to him again was progress, or simply the first of many nails waiting to be banged into his coffin.

* * *

ZOE SHOVED her belongings into the boxes she'd brought to the old, purple cottage two weeks ago.

How had she managed to transport and unpack so much in such little time? Everything was most definitely not going to fit into her adorable VW bug. There was no way. It had been shortsighted of her to have settled in despite knowing she could be turfed out at a moment's notice.

She sat heavily on the bed and fought tears.

She'd been turfed out by Ashton. Ashton and his wife.

And he'd come bearing a cinnamon bun from Sweet Caroline's.

A cinnamon bun, of all things! It was like he was trying to drive that wedge he'd placed in her heart all the way through. To remind her of what they'd once had before he'd gotten married.

She flopped backward on the mattress, bouncing lightly and upsetting her cat Binx, who stalked to her pillow, curling into a black ball.

Why had Ashton come back? Why here? Why now? He hadn't acted as though he believed the treat would make everything okay. It didn't matter, she reminded herself, because she wasn't forgiving him. He was like every other man she'd ever dated. He'd gone running for the hills—or in this case, the city—when she'd revealed the depths of her feelings, and the length of her intended commitment.

Why had he looked so sad, though? So stressed, almost beaten? And it wasn't just because of her rejection.

If he'd been any other man she would have brought him home and whipped up some comfort food—her grandmother's fried chicken, maybe, and an apple pie.

But he was Ashton and he didn't deserve a thing from her. Other than to fulfill her job of tending to his and his wife's needs as resort guests. And as a thank-you, she'd be treated to seeing them walking around hand in hand, kissing and laughing. All those things she used to do with Ashton, and had once believed she'd be doing for a lifetime.

She was going to throw up. Zoe moaned and rolled to a sitting position, letting the emotion fall away as she started packing again.

What did Ashton's wife look like, act like? And why did her husband seem so darn sad? What had happened to him?

And why had he chosen to come here, of all places—the resort where she worked?

Zoe thought about Dallas's claim that there was more to Ashton's story, as well as the reason he'd gone from one commitment to the next so quickly and unexpectedly. Maybe she hadn't been moving fast enough for him.

She let out a snort of disbelief. Not likely!

Anyway, it didn't matter. She had her own life, and he had his. She also had a cottage to clean for him and his perfect little wife, and less than an hour to do it, which so wasn't happening.

How much vacation time did she have saved up? Maybe she could run away like he had. Make up an excuse and go visit someone. Someone who didn't mind her bringing along five felines.

Zoe began shoving things into boxes again, half tempted to inconvenience Ashton and his bride by taking her time.

There was a knock at the door and she scrambled to wipe her damp eyes while hopscotching her way through the strewn boxes scattered over the wood floor. As she passed, Houdini, a gray tabby, hopped out of her open suitcase and dived into a cardboard box, then back out again when he discovered it was already occupied by a calico named Pandora.

The door swung open and for a moment Zoe thought it might be Vicky, the bartender from the resort's Tiki Hut bar, coming to help before her shift started. The cottages were like their own community, and info traveled faster than a pelican gave in to gravity when a fish was within its sights in the waters below. Maybe Vicky's landlord had let up on his no-cats rule and had an apartment Zoe could rent for a few weeks.

She caught sight of the person who'd entered. It wasn't Vicky. It was Ashton. His moves were fluid as he slipped inside, closing the door behind him and blocking Houdini just in time. He'd remembered the cat's escape abilities, something many of her friends often forgot or underestimated.

Zoe both loved and hated that he remembered.

He was the kind of man any woman would marry if given the chance.

She hadn't been given that chance, but someone else had.

She turned away, swallowing her bitterness. He still looked amazing. Forty-three, fit and...well, sad. His shoulders were sloped as though he was carrying a great load.

"I'll be out of here soon," Zoe said, grabbing a stack of books from the Christmas library sale off her dining room table. They hadn't been damaged in the flood, but she'd ended up hauling them here as though she'd expected them to become ruined if left behind. She didn't have anywhere to dump the books and set them down again.

"Margie at the desk told me your place flooded, and that you've been living here. I came to tell you not to pack. I'll stay at a hotel."

Mishka, normally an aloof puss, was rubbing against his legs, purring so loudly Zoe could hear it from across the room. Ashton reached down to scratch the cat behind the ears while Zoe kept packing.

Realizing she'd scooped up a pile of lingerie she'd laid out over the back of the couch to dry, she tossed the load into a suitcase at her feet, disturbing her overweight cat, Tiny, who tore through the room, the strap of a red lace bra caught around his neck. He tripped on the bra's cup, somersaulting before taking off again.

"Are you sure?" she asked Ashton. Finding somewhere that would take her and the cats wouldn't be easy.

"Yeah. It's just for a few months."

"A few months?" she asked weakly.

"I'll be filling in for a maternity leave at the elementary school starting in late August. I'm here until early November and I couldn't find any short-term leases."

I. Not we.

Was he divorced?

And if he was, did it matter?

She sighed and looked around the cottage. Nobody decent would let him stay in a hotel for four to five months, not when her boss could rent out the place she was squatting in. And anyway, summer was upon them and the rates were about to go through the roof. He needed to lock in a good deal now.

"You can't afford a hotel for that long," she said. He should stay here.

"Says who?"

"Is your wife rich? Or have they suddenly decided to pay teachers a whole lot more than they used to?" She ignored the way he'd flinched when she'd said "wife," and began stuffing possessions into boxes again. In the spare room she could hear scuffling, and she made a clicking noise to call whatever cat was no doubt destroying something she couldn't afford to replace.

The sound turned to choking.

Ashton was at the bedroom door before she could get there.

Tiny's back legs were scrambling for purchase on the wood floor, while the rest of him was hidden from view, caught behind the five-foot-wide wardrobe. The sound was coming from him.

Ashton reached the wardrobe first, and then Zoe fell to her knees beside it, trying to free the strangling cat, which was twisting and turning, obviously stuck. Ashton gripped the wardrobe, heaving it away from the wall one inch at a time. Its wooden feet screeched against the floor, panicking Tiny and causing the bra strap around his neck to cinch tighter as he tried to pull away.

"The strap's caught." Zoe reached beyond the writhing animal, a claw digging into her gut as she stretched to unhook the brassiere from the wardrobe's loose backing. But it was caught near the middle and her arm wasn't long enough to unhook it.

Then Ashton was leaning over her, his solid form pressing down on her as he reached through the gap between wardrobe and wall, freeing the garment. He smelled so familiar, and evoked such fond, warm memories, that her heart stung with loss.

Tiny, now released, turned and tore between Zoe's knees, the bra still wrapped around his neck.

"Catch him!" she called, scrambling backward.

Ashton took off after the cat, and by the time Zoe untangled herself and caught up with them he was on his belly, arms under the couch, gently talking to Tiny as he dragged him out of his hiding spot. The cat resisted, sinking his claws into Ashton's skin. Zoe winced, but Ashton remained calm as he continued to talk soothingly to the fat ball of fur wrapped around his hand.

Zoe moved forward and the cat hissed and writhed, making Ashton's job of unwinding the bra strap harder. She halted in her tracks as he gently untwisted the fabric. Tiny, free once again, set off across the room, sending an empty box flying that Pandora promptly jumped into.

Ashton sat back on his heels, the sadness in his eyes seeming so much larger in the shadows of her small living room.

"Your hands are a mess," she announced. *And you're holding my favorite bra.* A bra he'd purchased for her, in fact.

He looked down at his bleeding wrists, seeming almost

resigned to the pain. Noticing he was still holding the lacy piece of lingerie, he carefully set it aside, the sorrow in his eyes deepening.

Zoe hurried to the bathroom to wet a facecloth and gather what would do as a first aid kit. She returned to find Tiny sitting in a midafternoon sunbeam in her bedroom doorway, furiously licking his ruffled fur as though nothing life threatening had happened only moments ago, and he was merely miffed at his disheveled state.

Ashton had gone to the small kitchen and was running water over his wounds. He was different than the man she'd so quickly fallen in love with a year ago, and despite not wanting to, she found herself wondering what he'd been through, what his life was like now. Her best guess was that marriage wasn't suiting him. Did that mean she'd dodged a bullet?

"Thank you for saving Tiny," she said, as she drew one of Ashton's hands out from under the water and inspected it. His arm was warm and strong. Some of the cuts were still bleeding and she focused on them rather than the way it felt to be touching him, standing so close to him. If she could forgive the past she'd consider doing so for the sake of their former friendship.

She shook herself. What was she thinking? He'd broken her heart. She couldn't be friends with him after that.

Plus he was married. Wives didn't like their husband's ex-girlfriends hanging around. And ex-girlfriends didn't like wives who'd stolen away their man.

"It must sting," she said briskly, refocusing on the task before her. He didn't need stitches, but the scratches were definitely going to hurt for some time. He stood patiently, allowing her to dry his hands, then doctor him up, applying a healing cream that would also help disinfect the claw marks.

She smoothed bandages over the worst of them as they talked.

"Is Tiny okay?" he asked.

"I think so."

"It doesn't make sense for you to move out."

"It doesn't make sense for you to stay in a hotel." She saw him glance toward the second, currently vacant bedroom. "No."

"Why not?" he asked quietly.

"Because you're married!"

He shook his head. "I'm not." There was that sadness again, as well as something else. Anger?

"You said—"

"I'm no longer married," he stated rather sharply.

Why did that small fact take the fight out of her? And why did she feel relieved, of all things?

"And so now you're back." She looked up at him, trying to find her old anger, allow it to take root again and protect her, battle the curiosity and hope that had come—unwelcomed—out of left field.

Just because he was divorced didn't mean she was ready to forgive him, as well as overlook the way he'd hurt her.

"I'm back for now," he said.

"And expecting what?"

"I have no expectations, but I hope to mend fences. I owe you so much more than a simple apology."

She studied him for a long moment, his bandaged hand still in hers. She knew he meant every word. It was written in the resolve of his gaze, the tight, determined lines of his jaw. His peace offering of a cinnamon bun had been just that. As was his offer to stay in a hotel.

Genuine.

And the worst part was that she not only believed him, but she wanted to soften and forgive him. Just a little bit.

"I'm not ready to accept an apology." He'd made his choice when he'd married someone else. Zoe dropped her gaze to the bandages crisscrossing his skin. She released her grip on him and stuck her hands in the tiny back pockets of her dress pants, then took a step back.

"I understand," he said.

"So now what?"

"Now I try to make it up to you."

"I don't think I want that." She took another step back, but sent a cautious glance his way. His eyes were remorseful, full of sadness and longing.

Was it possible she'd somehow caused that sadness?

She shook the thought from her mind. He'd brought it upon himself, and letting him edge his way back into her life would only lead to more pain. And she'd had more than her fair share of that when it came to love.

CHAPTER 2

Ashton crawled out of the tent he'd pitched behind Zoe's cottage. They'd gone round and round about how to sort out their accommodation problem until finally they'd come to a temporary agreement. He'd camp out in her tent while trying not to suffocate in the humidity and pressing heat, and she and the cats would keep the cottage until they found a more permanent solution. Neither would tell Dallas, since technically Ashton was paying to stay *inside* the abode, and Zoe would likely get chewed out by her boss for ousting a paying guest.

Yes, Ashton was paying cottage rental rates to sleep in a stuffy old tent. He shook his head in amusement. He was really reaching, and that desperate for any softening from Zoe.

He peeled the bandages off his cat scratches and sat in the cold sand, squinting at the sliver of ocean visible from his spot, waiting for the sun to crawl higher in the sky before he went into the cottage to have a shower.

The beach and dunes surrounding him had a surreal

glow, and in the distance a sailboat floated by. An early riser out enjoying the calm waters.

He sure could go for a coffee.

Ashton glanced over his shoulder. The cottage's lights were still off, so he rolled up the tent and sleeping bag, tucked them on the porch, then pulled a ball cap over his bed head and made his way to Sweet Caroline's for breakfast and coffee.

As he approached the blue awning above the café's picture window, he inhaled deeply, catching a hint of the bracing aroma of roasted coffee beans. When he entered, Caroline, a woman in her late fifties, glanced up, breaking into a smile of recognition.

"Look who the cat dragged in. Ashton Wallace! Didn't think I'd see you again."

"You're as pretty as ever," he told her.

She waved off the compliment. "How long are you here for?"

"November. I'm filling in for Sandra at the elementary school."

"I heard a rumor you were in yesterday buying a cinnamon bun. Who'd you share it with?" She gave him a sly look. She knew last summer's routine, where he'd stop in at two forty-five to purchase a pastry to share with Zoe during her coffee break.

"My peace offering was rejected."

Caroline placed a palm over her heart and frowned sympathetically. "Well, these things take time." Then she dropped her hands on her hips, her sympathy gone. "Besides, I heard you went and got married."

She wasn't impressed with him and there was no doubt as to why—he and Zoe had seemed like a sure thing. So sure that he hadn't quite believed the quick change in his life last August when he'd found himself wed to someone else. The year and a half he'd lived in Indigo Bay had been the best he'd ever spent, and the town had felt like home. However, he wasn't sure the community would welcome him back. When you walked out on a hometown gal, people didn't take too kindly to you. No matter what your reasons were or how valid they felt at the time.

"I did," he said, in answer to her statement.

"And?"

"I'm widowed."

Caroline tilted her head to the side in sympathy. "Well, bless your heart, sweet pea. I'm sorry to hear that."

The loss of his wife wasn't the worst of what Ashton had been through since he'd been away, and his anger surfaced once again, like an old unwanted friend. Although maybe that didn't make it a friend.

"Well, whatever you do, don't tell Miss Lucille about your new status," Caroline teased gently. "She'd love nothing more than to match you up with her great-niece Maggie, who must be close to faking a husband by now just to dodge her aunt's persistent matchmaking."

Caroline didn't ask for details about Ashton's late wife, but he could see the questions in her eyes. What had happened? Why had he married her? Why had he broken Zoe's heart? Had Zoe been the woman on the side? But the biggest question was why he'd returned.

"You and I will talk later," Caroline promised, as another customer came in, a local officer who'd once pulled Ashton over for speeding to the cottages with a cinnamon bun the day he'd got caught up in a good mystery and had forgotten the time.

"Good morning, Caroline," Officer Ben Andrews said, nodding a hello to Ashton. Caroline began fixing the man's coffee to go without being asked. "Do you know who owns a late model Ford Escape? Black. Tinted windows."

"Tinted windows? Not Tandy from the cottages then." She twisted her lips in thought. "Out of towner?"

"Must be. Parked in a yellow zone." Ben accepted the takeout cup from Caroline and moseyed toward the door. "The vehicle seems like it's been everywhere in town over the past twenty-four hours."

"Well, if the windows aren't tinted as dark as a drug dealer's, then it's probably a tourist." She shook her head, then called after him, "Send them here if they're hungry!" She turned to Ashton. "Are you ordering breakfast?"

He pointed to the pot of freshly brewed coffee, exposing his scratched hand in the process. She clucked and reached for his wrist. "Hon, it looks like you got something madder than a wet hen."

Ashton self-consciously tucked the hand in his back pocket. "I was rescuing Zoe's cat."

"My word. From what?"

"He got tangled in her…undergarments."

Caroline raised her eyebrows as she poured him a cup of coffee. "Maybe these things don't take time, after all."

Ashton chuckled. "Just laundry. Don't get your hopes up." Like his. He had to keep them on a tether or they would float away without him.

She winked, pushing the cup across the counter. "I was rooting for you—but only for Zoe's sake. I don't appreciate how you ran out on her when things were getting serious. But you two were good together, and she missed you when you left. There's a lid for every pot, hon, and I believe in second chances."

"I missed her, too."

"Don't hurt her, and don't blow it this time." She shook her finger at him.

Ashton nodded quickly, doubtful Zoe would let him anywhere near her heart ever again, and placed the rest of his breakfast order. He then went to sit at the table by the window, where he used the café's Wi-Fi to download a book on creating email newsletters. He took his time enjoying his breakfast, certain Zoe would appreciate him staying out of her hair over at the cottage as she got ready for work.

Before he left, he ordered a cinnamon bun to go. He was determined before the month was out that he and Zoe would share one. Maybe not quite like old times, but as friends. And maybe it would help heal over the hole he'd left in her heart last August.

But at some point he was going to have to reveal the truth of the past, and suffer judgment for how he'd failed her as well as himself.

* * *

ZOE HAD SNEAKED off to work before dawn. She'd been worried that if she saw Ashton all sleepy-eyed from his night in the tent, she might cave and let him sleep in the cottage. Or make him a hearty breakfast to remove any chill from sleeping outdoors.

He was single again. He'd come back to Indigo Bay.

He'd also ripped her heart out when he'd run off to marry someone else, so how could her heart still have hope?

But what if he'd divorced his wife because she hadn't been Zoe, and he'd missed having her wrapped in his arms each night?

As a result of her hope she'd spent five extra minutes in the bathroom that morning taking special care with her makeup and shoulder-length hair even though it didn't matter. Couldn't, shouldn't matter.

She was determined to continue to find ways to avoid him. Last night she'd hovered around one of the resort's weddings despite Hope Ryan having everything under control from hanging her gorgeous seascape panels in the multi-purpose room, to the eighty unique party favors she'd created for guests. Honestly, Zoe didn't know how she'd ever gotten by before hiring her as an assistant. Hope couldn't help with the newsletter though, and so Zoe had come to work early and researched everything she'd needed to know about creating the emails, in order to send off the first one just before ten.

Not bad for a newbie.

And with no help from Ashton, either.

Zoe pushed back from her desk and rolled the crick out of her right shoulder. She spotted a familiar face approaching and rose to her feet with a smile.

"I saw your name on the reservation list! Welcome back." Zoe came around the desk to give Ginger McGinty a giant hug, happy to see last year's returning guest. Well, except for the fact that the matchmaker from Blueberry Springs had been the one to push her and Ashton together, and would naturally want an update. And after the update, she'd learn that Ashton was back, and would likely want to meddle.

"You're here?" Ginger said with surprise.

"Where else would I be?"

She shook her head, her auburn hair bouncing. "I heard something from Caroline Harper this morning and—never mind. I must have leaped to a conclusion." She hugged Zoe again.

"Where's Logan?" Zoe asked, referring to Ginger's husband. Zoe had helped the two quick-to-wed elope at the resort last spring.

"He's not coming."

Her joy over seeing Ginger turned to concern. "Oh, I'm sorry."

Maybe her friend wouldn't want to chat about relationships, after all.

"No, nothing like that. My business has been going great guns since the workshops I took here at last year's wedding expo, and I needed some time away to regroup and strategize. I'm months behind on assessing my business plan and crunching the data to see where I need to go next. I kept thinking of Indigo Bay and that sweet little honeymoon cottage. So Logan urged me to come here to focus on my plans."

"How is he?"

"Good. Really good. He's started a business in town with his friend Zach Forrester, doing security stuff, and his daughter has fallen in love."

If Zoe recalled correctly, Annabelle had some mental development delays, and had been in assisted living here in Indigo Bay. After Logan and Ginger married, they'd all moved to Blueberry Springs.

"It's not requited love, unfortunately, and she's having a tough go. But there's this really sweet guy at the recycling center who has his eye on her, and I'm hoping something happens. In the meantime, Logan is fretting over her."

"Tell them both hello from me, and I hope things work out well in the love department." Zoe didn't know the whole story of how Logan became Annabelle's dad, only that he'd stepped in as her guardian, and somewhere along the line had legally adopted her.

"I'm going to miss Logan while I'm here, but having no distractions will be perfect." Ginger propped her fingertips together, her gold-and-green wedding band catching the light. "So? How about you?" She saw Zoe eyeing her ring, and snatched up Zoe's left hand, frowning at her bare finger. "I heard Ashton's a recent widow, and yet here you are...very much alive."

Zoe's fingers flew to her mouth as she held in a gasp of surprise.

A widow?

That changed everything.

No. No, it didn't.

He hadn't divorced someone to come back to Zoe. He wasn't here because it hadn't worked out, or because he'd secretly been dreaming of her, knowing he'd made a mistake. He had still chosen the other woman over her. And now she was gone, so he was back.

"And yet here you are...alive," Ginger mused again, eyebrows raised.

Zoe pulled herself from her thoughts. "Oh, right. He broke up with me, and then married...her."

Ginger's jaw dropped. "No!"

Zoe nodded. "Pretty much immediately." She tried to swallow the lump of emotion that had formed in her throat.

"Was she pregnant?"

Did it matter? He'd been talking about heavy commitment things with Zoe—move in together, foster or adopt some kids, live happily ever after...and then boom. He was gone. Off marrying someone else.

Zoe took a stack of papers from her desk and gave them a sharp whack to straighten them.

Even if Ashton's late wife had been pregnant, it wouldn't have been enough to cause him to change directions so suddenly. He longed for a family, just as Zoe did, and she knew he would do anything in his power to avoid becoming a deadbeat dad like his father, but that didn't equal marriage. It had to have been something more. And despite everything, Zoe was curious to know what had caused his abrupt about-face. Well, unless it made her anger seem unfair and irrational. Because she knew she needed to hold on to her anger so she wouldn't get hurt again.

"Huh," Ginger said thoughtfully, when she didn't respond. "I was certain you two were a sure thing."

So had she. And as far as she could figure, she'd done everything right when he'd asked for space. She hadn't smothered him with questions, hadn't pried. She'd been patient. But instead of Ashton coming back to her, he'd run down the aisle with someone else.

"He just came back to town yesterday," Zoe said, surprised to find herself offering more information. "He's filling in for a maternity leave until November."

"And looking for a second chance?" Ginger perched her hip on the edge of Zoe's desk.

"No," she replied sharply.

"Then why is he back—and a few months before school starts—if not for you? You loved him once."

"He proved he didn't love me."

"What if there's some tragic story there? This woman he married—what if she was deathly ill and he married her because otherwise her children would be sent to the orphanage and—"

"No."

"No? I guess kids don't get sent to orphanages any longer," Ginger mused. "Do you still care for him?"

"Does it matter?"

"That's not a no," Ginger pointed out, smiling at a familiar figure moving through the lobby.

It was Ashton. Why was Zoe not surprised to see him glancing her way nervously, while toying with a box from Sweet Caroline's?

* * *

ASHTON KEPT himself busy looking at old resort photos lining the wall until Ginger, the woman who had originally brought him and Zoe together, walked off with a wink and a wave.

"I brought you something for your coffee break," he said, when he reached Zoe's desk. He set the bun in front of her.

With a gentle, but firm look, she said, "I told you—"

"You can throw it out if you want."

He saw her hesitate, the pastry box clutched so tightly in her hands that the lid buckled. Something had changed since he'd seen her last night. In place of that wall she'd erected was something akin to compassion and curiosity. Why?

"You already apologized," she murmured. She slid the container his way. "And I'm not interested in taking you back."

"I didn't ask you to."

He waited for that to sink in, wondering why she was acting so careful instead of ticked off.

"I sent the first newsletter this morning. It wasn't too difficult to figure out." She tipped up her chin and turned away from him. "Consider yourself off the hook."

"Any questions I can answer?"

"You can answer this," trilled a prim voice from behind Ashton. He turned to find Lucille Sanderson in her high heels, waving a piece of paper, her fluffy dog trailing behind on a loose, thin leash.

"Good morning, Miss Lucille," Zoe said, her expression pleasant. "What can I do for you today?"

"Why are you sending me emails?" demanded the older woman. Her blond hair—thanks to help from her hairdresser —was in a loose bun, her trim and trendy look belying her seventy-some years. She smacked down a piece of paper with the resort's logo on it. It was a printed copy of Zoe's newsletter, its template a bit skewed, so the paragraph columns ran long and narrow, taking up several pages.

It looked like Zoe might need some help, after all.

"Before you say a word, Ashton," Zoe said coolly, "I have this."

Yeah, she didn't have it. And that small fact provided him with hope.

"Why am I getting this?" Lucille tapped the paper with a polished nail. "Why do I need to hear about resort deals? I'm not going to pay good money to stay in a place minutes from my home."

"If you have guests they might be interested in staying here."

"Are you suggesting I'm too old to provide hospitality for my guests?"

"No." Zoe's cheeks grew pink. "The newsletter I sent you is about a refer-a-friend to our spa deal. I thought you might enjoy a manicure." Zoe turned the newsletter to face her, scanning it as though looking for the paragraph with the offer. She frowned.

"I get my nails done at Indigo Bay Nails and More," Lucille said. "You know that. Rochelle is a member of the Ashland Belle Society. How would it look if I started coming here?"

"Rochelle does most of our spa treatments on contract," Zoe explained. She handed the newsletter back to the woman. "I'm sorry, Miss Lucille. I'll fix whatever went wrong so you get the local pampering and restaurant deals instead of the one for rooms."

"I don't need deals! I'm doing just fine financially, thank you, and I don't want your emails. I'll hire a smart lawyer like Lauren Cooper and sue you for harassment!"

"Miss Lucille," Ashton said carefully, feeling it was time to step in. "We're sorry for the error. Please be assured that we will fix it."

"*We?* Is there a 'we' happening here once again?" she asked, turning on him, her bright eyes flashing. "If I recall, which I do perfectly well, you left this woman high and dry." Lucille's dog, Princess, let out a sharp bark as though backing up her owner. "What gall you have, showing your face around here after that! Every night I thank my lucky stars I didn't set you up with my great-niece Maggie." She sniffed.

"Miss Lucille…" Zoe said uneasily.

"He lost you a nonrefundable deposit on a moving company you never used. Am I the only person who remembers that?"

"It was premature of me to book them," Zoe said, her eyes cast down and to the side. "And Ashley Harden was able to use the moving company when she moved to Florida to be with Will Layton, so all was not lost."

Lucille tsked, her nose held high.

"Lesson learned and all of that," Zoe added quietly.

Ashton felt as though someone had pushed him underwater. He couldn't breathe, thinking about how Zoe had truly been left, as Lucille put it, high and dry. Because of him.

"Is there a problem here?" Dallas asked, joining them. "Miss Lucille. Wonderful to see you." He glanced down at the dog, who was sniffing about as though on the lookout for a place to relieve herself. "And Princess. She looks like she needs to go outside. Shall we take her to our doggy zone?"

Lucille started ranting at Dallas about the newsletter, and he apologized, while smoothly guiding her and the pooch outdoors. He muttered over his shoulder before he left, "I told you to use Ash's help."

Zoe shot Ashton a dark look.

"You have a lot on your plate," he said simply, then pulled a chair from a nearby workstation and sat himself near her computer. "Shall we see what went wrong with your segmentation?"

"I segmented it just fine. So don't try and fix things. It's broken. Forever."

His proximity seemed to be making her agitated, and he

settled in a little closer to note the effect. She pushed up her cardigan's sleeves despite the building's robust air conditioning.

"I know," he said softly. "I'm sorry. And I'm sorry about the movers."

He'd been wrong, slipping away last August instead of trying to awkwardly make things work, or telling her every gory detail of the mess he'd landed himself in. He could see that he hadn't prevented additional hurt like he'd believed he was doing. In fact, he'd quite possibly caused her even more distress, as well as public humiliation, if someone like Lucille Sanderson was nattering on about their failed love life.

He opened his mouth, then closed it again, uncertain what to say beyond the fact that he was sorry. So sorry.

Zoe had pulled up the newsletter program and was clicking her way through various setup options. "I don't know why Lucille got the wrong email. I'm sure I did it all correctly. But even if I did mess up, Lauren will talk Lucille out of suing."

"I wanted to ask earlier; is she related to Josh Cooper?"

"Who?" Zoe frowned at the screen. "Lucille?"

"Lauren. Josh's a famous sportscaster who's big into football."

"What?" She squinted at him. "No. That's Hope's boyfriend—well, they're taking a break or something. But anyway, why does everyone always assume he and Lauren are related?"

"Because he's famous and it would be cool."

Zoe returned her attention to the computer monitor, sighing dejectedly, her shoulders curving forward.

"How do I undo that?" she asked, pointing at her mistake.

"You can't."

"But I need to unsend it."

"No can do. Newsletters are like life mistakes. You can't

undo them."

Zoe sent him with a skeptical, unimpressed look.

"You just have to apologize sincerely," he said, "and move forward, hoping for the best."

"Is that what you're doing? Hoping for the best?"

He wanted to meet her frank, open gaze—he'd always appreciated her directness when they'd been moving fast with their relationship—but right now it felt like a knife nudging at tender bruises. Maybe he wasn't ready to shoulder the knowledge of just how much he'd hurt her. Maybe he wasn't ready to forgive himself for making the wrong choice last summer, as well as for excluding her from his decisions for fear of her blowing the legal whistle on his and Maliki's marriage-for-medical-insurance arrangement.

"Ashton? Is it?" Zoe prodded.

He might not get a second chance to have this conversation.

"Yes," he said.

"And what if your "hope for the best" differs from what I'm hoping for?" She was looking straight at him, her right hand resting on the computer mouse, her tone gentle despite her bluntness.

"I shouldn't have shut you out. I should have told you…" He wanted to tell her what she needed to hear, but couldn't. "I know you wanted me to tell you everything, and I didn't."

"It's too late, Ashton." She pushed away from the computer. "You made a choice. You didn't trust me or love me enough to let me in, and that's an important thing in a relationship." She was standing over him. "Your actions negated everything you said to me, and spewing sweet nothings now won't make up for that."

She stormed off, making Ashton wish he had a time machine so he could go back and make a better choice. The right choice.

CHAPTER 3

Zoe stopped on the sidewalk in front of her house, unsure whether to march off or stick around and satisfy her curiosity. She'd come by to check on the flood repairs, as well as to dig her picnic basket out of the stuffed portable storage unit the insurance company had placed in her front yard. Whitney from Coastal Creations was hoping to borrow it if Zoe could find it.

But there in her front yard was Ashton, covered in dirt, shovel in hand.

"What are you doing?" Zoe asked.

"Keeping my promise." He leaned against the shovel, casual and handsome.

The half-dead front hedge that she'd always meant to do something about had been entirely removed. A pickup truck she recognized as belonging to Dallas was piled high with brush and branches.

Of all Ashton's promises, this wasn't the one Zoe had set her heart on him keeping.

"Remember our plan?" Ashton pulled a piece of paper from his back pocket, marking the paper with grubby fingerprints. He unfolded the landscaping plan they'd mapped out at her kitchen table the year before.

"You're going to make me a gazebo, create a rosebush front hedge and a stone walkway?" she asked in disbelief.

He nodded.

She waved toward her damaged house. "The deductible ate my landscaping fund. I can't afford it."

And you left me, making all your promises a moot point.

Ashton tucked the piece of paper into his back pocket once again. "Then we'll wait on the gazebo. I can afford the rest."

She wanted to reject him outright, send him away, but she held her tongue until the first wave of anger had passed. "You have no right to do this. You are no longer a part of my life, my world." Her palms hurt, and she realized she'd squeezed her hands into fists, her nails digging into her own flesh.

"I want to do this," he stated.

"What if I don't want you buying me roses?" Roses felt romantic, and his gesture was too big, too kind. It was difficult to remain as angry as she wanted to be when he was being so careful, so…Ashton.

"I figured as much. I thought you might prefer camellias, as they're evergreen, hardy, and bloom while everything else has gone dormant."

Of course he'd thought out all the angles.

Dejectedly, Zoe stared at her home. The plan for the garden had been to create a haven for her to read in after work, a nice place to eat together when it wasn't too hot out. But then they'd started talking about moving in together, choosing a bigger house over either of the places they had been living, so they could start a family via fostering or adopting children, as she was past her prime childbearing years. And so they had spun a different dream, abandoning the idea of creating a landscaped paradise in her yard.

A power saw screeched and workers chucked yet more of her home's interior into the trash bin on the lawn. Why now? How did Ashton believe this was a good time to rip up the one thing in her life that wasn't in shambles? She couldn't deal with this. Every time she looked at her house she wanted to cry, and having a ditch where her hedge used to be didn't help.

She shook her head and turned, walking back toward the Indigo Bay Cottages. He'd left her, left this dream behind. And him taking it up right now only seemed to rub in the fact that she would always live alone in this small bungalow and never a large and boisterous family home.

This wasn't supposed to be her life. This wasn't where she'd been hoping to be at age forty-one.

Ashton's footsteps echoed on the sidewalk as he hurried to catch up with her. She hugged her arms tighter around her torso, bent her head and walked faster.

"I'm sorry," he said. "I was afraid you were going to say no if I asked."

"And why would I ever say yes?" she asked, spinning around to face him. "Don't you get it? You left me. You walked out on us—on you and me. You chose someone else despite everything we'd talked about."

He had dirt on his nose, and his eyes were filled with such remorse that she didn't know whether to shout or cry.

"I'm sorry," he said.

"Quit apologizing."

"I will when I stop screwing up."

"You're going to be underfoot until I say I forgive you, aren't you?"

"I was stupid to leave you."

"Then why did you? Why did you—" She caught herself and took a deep breath. It didn't matter. Not anymore.

Ashton didn't answer as he used the toe of his shoe to

trace a line through the beach sand that had filtered in after the last storm, coating part of the sidewalk. Normally, she would have swept it away by now.

"I missed out on something special when I..." He paused and peeked up at her, his hazel eyes so sincere. "I made the wrong choice even though I thought I was doing the right thing."

"Why? Was she pregnant?" Zoe scrunched her eyes shut and shook her head. "No, I don't want to know."

The less she knew, the less she had as ammo for torturing herself with what-if's.

Ashton's throat was working as though he was struggling to remember how to breathe or talk.

"This isn't going to cause me to forgive you," she said, gesturing toward her destroyed yard. "Finish what you started by the time I move back in two weeks, and don't you dare leave me with a mess. This time follow through on your promises."

* * *

ASHTON SLAMMED the shovel into the dry earth. Why couldn't he get it right? Why couldn't he just open his mouth and tell her everything like he used to? What was he afraid of? Her running to his medical company and telling them he'd married Maliki for coverage? He'd already done the worst thing he could think of by shutting Zoe out of his life, and by leaving her.

Why had he let her storm away just now? Why hadn't he told her the truth?

Because he'd rather look like a hurtful ex-lover than a man who had been played like a fool. He'd rather forget the pain of the past, the deception that had caught him in its snare, and move forward, fresh and new. The only way to move on was to leave the past where it belonged—in the past.

But was he really choosing Zoe's scorn over pity? It hurt, knowing he'd failed her so spectacularly, and that he still caused her so much pain.

Maybe he should tell the school he couldn't fulfill the maternity leave contract and go back to Charleston. Let Zoe have some much-wanted peace, and give up on his quest.

He bent over, hands on his knees, the heat of the day suddenly draining him of energy and motivation.

No. He had to finish this job. He needed to show Zoe through his actions that he still cared, and that she was still important to him. Because without her in his life there wasn't much worth living for. He walked his hands up his thighs, straightening up once again.

"Why are you doing this?"

Ashton gave a start at the unexpected question. Zoe had returned, hands on her hips, brow furrowed.

She'd come back, like the second chance he'd been wishing for. He sent a silent prayer to the sky above before blurting out, "She was."

Maliki, his ex-girlfriend, had been pregnant. That was the answer to the question Zoe had asked before storming off, after he'd frozen up, fearing her judgment, unable to answer. Unable to go down that road so filled with anguish.

"She was what?" Zoe asked carefully.

"Pregnant."

Zoe's hands fell loose at her sides as comprehension dawned. "Oh."

"Yeah." He kicked the shovel into the dirt, lifting a cracked block of the sidewalk that led to Zoe's front door.

"And now she's…gone," Zoe said carefully. "Where's the baby?"

"Turns out she wasn't mine." Ashton felt the rage of

betrayal and usury settle in once again. He gripped the shovel's handle so he wouldn't hurl it across the yard in a rage. The cat scratches on his hands had scabbed and puckered, itching like mad, and he wanted to tear them open, feel the pain somewhere other than in his heart for the way he'd lost Zoe by stepping up and doing what he'd believed was the right thing. Maliki had overturned his life and stolen moments he'd never get back, because he'd been a sucker. He'd fallen for her woes and convinced himself it would work out and be okay because he was a nice guy.

A nice guy.

They always finished last.

"Ashton?"

He waited a long few seconds before looking up at Zoe.

"I don't understand."

He closed his eyes as bitter betrayal and anger washed over him. He hadn't understood, either.

"Jaelyn is nine months old and living with her real dad."

"I thought you were going to marry me," Zoe said, her voice shaking with emotion. "Then you left without explaining. You shut me out. We could have gotten through this together."

The word *together* settled like an impossible weight on his shoulders. Or maybe that was just a heavy dose of guilt for trying to spare her, for shielding her—and failing.

"I was trying to protect you," he said hoarsely. Zoe had been so quiet last summer when he'd told her he had to go to the city to work out some stuff. She hadn't been nosy or prodded him into talking like he'd expected, and a part of him had thought that maybe she was secretly relieved to be given some space.

"No," she insisted, "that's called not trusting me, or the strength of our relationship. You didn't trust me to help you, to confide in me. Instead you married...*her*. You found someone else to have a family with. I thought you loved me. I thought our plan was what you wanted." She stopped, swallowing hard, her eyes damp.

Ashton felt his shoulders drop. "I...I was trying to do the right thing. It wasn't about you." It hadn't even been about him. It had been about giving that child a chance in a medical situation where everything could be lost so quickly.

"Exactly." Zoe snatched the shovel from him and threw it on the ground at his feet. "I thought we were more than just two individuals when we were together. I thought we were partners." She swallowed hard, her eyes so wet he knew tears would fall at any moment.

"We were," he managed to choke out. There was still so much to explain, so much to convey, but it felt so futile and meaningless in the light of her pain. He'd dreamed that he and Zoe would help raise the child together. And then everything had changed, so severely, in that one simple conversation with Maliki that he hadn't known which way was up any longer, only that he had to step in and help or he would lose everything. More than just Zoe.

But in the end, he'd lost it all.

"I didn't mean to hurt you," he insisted.

"Why are you back in Indigo Bay?"

He ignored her question. "I didn't know Jaelyn wasn't mine until after Maliki died and Jaelyn's real father came to claim her." Ashton had fought for her for months and lost, and he still couldn't figure out why it hurt so badly, when she'd never even been his. "I was played, Zoe. I was played, and you and I lost everything, and I will always be eternally sorry for that." To his horror, he felt his own eyes dampen. He closed them, struggling for control. "I came here because...because I just wanted..."

Forgiveness.

A second chance. A do-over.

And it was too much to ask. He could see that now.

To his surprise he felt arms snake their way around him. Despite knowing he would make Zoe's sunny-yellow shirt dirty, he hugged her tight, promising himself he'd never let her go, never take a day or a grain of forgiveness or understanding for granted ever again.

* * *

THE NEXT DAY, when Ashton showed up at Zoe's work carrying a box from Sweet Caroline's, she was unable to prevent her old fight-or-flight reaction from kicking in. She smoothed her hands over the cool surface of her desk and calmed her heart rate. Ashton smiled tentatively, doing nothing to help slow her pulse.

She couldn't do this. She couldn't forgive him. And yet when he smiled like that, all uncertain and wounded, it felt possible. Like she could. It didn't help that yesterday she'd felt such sympathy for him she'd ended up embracing him in a giant hug, one that had felt so right.

But it still hurt. He'd shut her out rather than telling her the truth last summer. He hadn't allowed her to help him deal with how his life was changing, and that still mattered to her. It also revealed that there had been a giant communication hole in their relationship.

Last night, in another fit of avoidance, she'd spent hours walking the beach, then dining out with Ginger instead of facing Ashton and his grief. She knew how much he wanted a family. But why hadn't he told her his ex was expecting? Why had he married her?

Zoe had to still be missing a chunk of the puzzle. A piece beyond the fact that Ashton was the most giving, thoughtful man she knew. He'd been taken advantage of by a woman who'd used him, lied to him, and as a result ruined everything for Zoe and Ashton. If the woman had still been alive, Zoe would have finished her off herself.

And now, thanks to Ashton's late wife, she had conflicting feelings of wanting to both console Ashton and smack him upside the head for shutting her out and marrying such a woman.

So she'd come in to work early again today to avoid him at the cottage, and he'd arrived in time for her afternoon coffee break, as was their new routine.

Ashton set the box on her desk. He was dressed in old jeans and a T-shirt stained with dirt.

"Good afternoon," he said.

"Are you still working on my yard?" It didn't feel quite right that he was doing her landscaping.

"I am," he said.

"You don't have to." It was difficult to hang on to her anger when he was trying so hard to make things right again by breaking his back in her tired old yard.

He simply smiled and stepped back from her desk. "I hope you enjoy your break."

Then he turned on his heel and walked outside, hands in his pockets.

Zoe gaped after him. That was not what she had expected him to do.

He was wooing her.

No, looking for forgiveness.

But it felt a lot like wooing.

A slow, careful wooing.

She wasn't certain how that made her feel.

Special? Wary? A little bit excited?

She opened the small box, inhaling the sweet scent of sugar and cinnamon. Once again bittersweet memories washed over her and she set the box aside, the treat untouched. She needed to stay calm, stay the course.

What was her course, again?

Not move too fast.

No, not that.

Stand firm. He still hadn't explained everything. It had been a struggle for him to admit all that he had last night, but she knew there was still more.

"Is that fresh from Sweet Caroline's?" asked Kelso, one of the guys on staff, as he passed her desk.

Zoe lifted the box without looking. "Take it."

"Really?" He grinned like she'd made his day. "No matter what everyone says, Zoe, you're the best."

"Very funny," she said drily.

She turned to her computer, staring at her monitor, her mind tumbling. She picked up a pencil to try and train her thoughts on one thing at a time. She still couldn't get over the way Ashton had been betrayed and used by his ex—who had since passed away. How had he so easily and quickly been pulled back into a relationship with her? And what had caused her to pass on?

The pencil Zoe was holding snapped and she took a calming breath.

It didn't help. She wanted to break another pencil. An entire case of them.

She growled at her computer, then jumped when someone cleared his throat.

"Is this a bad time?" It was the man who'd come by the other day asking about a guest.

"Not at all," she said brightly. "What can I assist you with?"

"Has Quentin Valant checked in yet?" He took a folded handkerchief from a back pocket of his jeans and dabbed at his forehead.

"Hot out there today?" Zoe asked, as she checked the reservations list. She shivered as he put his handkerchief back in his pocket. There was something about him today that felt off—and not just the fact that he was carrying a handkerchief like a proper gentleman when she could see tattoos creeping above his shirt's neckline toward his chin. The man didn't add up.

"Muggy."

"Hmm. There's still no reservation under that name. Maybe he's decided to stay elsewhere?"

"Maybe."

"Would there be another name I could search under?"

The man gave her a thoughtful look. "Maybe I'll give him another day, but thanks for your help."

Zoe answered a few emails after he left, then finished her shift and headed back to the cottage, her footsteps slowing as she grew closer.

"Hey," Ashton said. He was coming around the side of the cottage, filthy from head to toe and looking exhausted.

"Need a shower?" As per their deal, he had use of the cottage bathroom and kitchen even though he was sleeping in the tent.

"I was thinking I'd take a swim in the ocean. Care to join me?"

Zoe turned to take in the lazily rolling Atlantic, then glanced back at Ashton. He looked wiped. If she didn't go with him she'd likely spend the time worrying he was drowning.

And a swim did feel tempting. The day was muggy and a thin layer of sweat had gathered over her while she was walking home. Plus she couldn't help but think that spending more time with Ashton might encourage him to open up, and spill some of the secrets she knew he was still keeping.

"Sure," she said hesitantly. "Why not?"

Ashton ran up the porch steps to go get changed into his swimming trunks. "Last one in is a dirty rotten egg!"

Where had that burst of energy come from?

"Oh yeah?" Zoe called, accepting his challenge. She waited for him to turn, then sprinted across the beach toward the ocean, unbuttoning her blouse as she ran. She was wearing a dark camisole underneath and let the blouse drop to the sand. She dared a glance over her shoulder. Ashton had been watching, taken off guard, but now was in hot pursuit, discarding his own shirt.

Zoe shrieked with the thrill of competition, and raced to the packed wet sand along the shoreline. She was wearing cotton golf shorts, which would hold up in the seawater just fine. She was totally going to win this one. She bent to quickly undo the straps of her leather sandals, tossing them behind her where they wouldn't be swept away by the waves or ruined by the salty spray. As she did, Ashton tore past her, hitting the water, waves breaking against his thighs as he arched over one, diving below the surface.

"Are you kidding me?" Zoe said when he came up for air. She'd made it knee deep and was clearly the dirty rotten egg despite her head start.

He was grinning, looking more free than he had since his arrival in town. "Maybe next time, slowpoke."

She scowled, feeling miffed. "Have you been exercising? You didn't used to be able to run that fast." He was standing waist-deep, pushing his way toward her, water streaming off him. He had definitely been working out. His chest was rippled, his waist more defined.

She liked what she saw, which unsettled her. Too many memories. Too many more that she wanted create after drinking him in.

"You're still dry," he pointed out as he neared her.

"Not for long." She quickly dived to the right, plunging under before he could reach her. She kicked, letting the saltwater buoy her to the surface several feet away. It was so refreshing, and just what she'd needed.

She stood, letting the water rush out of her clothes. It was time to head back to shore and get a shirt back on her ex so it was easier to remember all the reasons she wanted to keep him at a distance. She pulled her camisole away from her body, conscious of how it was clinging.

Ashton splashed her playfully. "You're beautiful. Quit fussing."

She turned, giving him a look that suggested he didn't have the right to compliment her, and was caught off guard by the way he was wistfully admiring her.

He splashed her again and she splashed back, letting her past hurt and anger fuel her actions, until it felt like an outright war. Therapeutic and fun. Saltwater stung her eyes and she dug her hands through the waves, dousing him over and over until she ached from the effort. Then she laughed and turned her back to the waves of water he sent her way. A family was swimming nearby and Ashton accidentally splashed them in his quest to get her.

He called out an apology to the family, as Zoe turned to him, shoving playfully. "Don't you have any manners?" she scolded.

"No. Do you?"

"Sometimes. I just don't reserve them for you," she replied, giving him a teasing glance.

He brushed at her shoulder, his expression tender, cautious. "You know the best way to get all this sand off?"

"A shower," she said, moving away again in case he had ideas about dunking her under the waves.

"Nope." He made a lunge for her, missing when she sidestepped at the last moment.

She laughed, feeling light and bubbly. When Ashton surfaced, she splashed him again and he raised his arms, resembling a sea monster as he came at her once again. Helpless with laughter now, she let him catch her. But instead of pulling her under, he held her tight, their warm, wet bodies pressed together.

Their eyes met and a moment passed as they gazed at each other. Zoe's palms were against Ashton's chest, his body snugged to hers.

It felt good. Too good.

She averted her eyes and swam away.

For a moment she'd thought they were going to kiss.

And she wasn't ready for that.

Not by a long shot.

* * *

ASHTON STILL HAD MORE to tell Zoe about why he'd left, but he was afraid to upset the new balance they were quickly establishing. They'd had fun in the ocean, their water fight a release for some of their emotions, and had come back to the cottage to dry off, then flop onto the couch in front of the TV. There was a cheesy John Candy movie on from the 1980s and they'd settled in front of it without question. Just like old times. At one point Zoe had dialed in an order for a pepperoni and mushroom pizza, half with pineapple for her. Again, just like old times.

They'd eaten, watched, and eventually she'd fallen asleep next to him, drifting against his side as time passed, Mishka, the Persian, curled next to her.

He'd flipped to the sports channel, and had no intention of ever getting up off this couch again. Not until Zoe did first.

Something rough brushed his ear and he flinched. It was Tiny, perched on the back of the couch, licking his earlobe.

Zoe stretched. "Did I miss the ending?" She caught herself

leaning against him and straightened so quickly the cat beside her went scurrying.

"Yeah."

She stood, clearing her throat, her eyes settling everywhere but on him. "I'm going to call it a night."

"Thanks for the evening." It felt formal thanking her, but he knew he was a long ways off from doing what he really wanted, which was to pull her into his arms and kiss her. He almost had in the ocean, but it was too soon. It might forever be too soon.

"It was...nice." Zoe suddenly looked shy, and Ashton took his cue. Exit before things got weird and awkward. An uncertain truce was a godsend at this point, and he'd do whatever it took to avoid messing up.

"Good night." He headed for the porch, where the tent was stored.

"Ashton?"

Her urgent tone caused him to turn, look to his feet in case a cat—namely Houdini—was trying to make a beeline for the door. There was no cat. Ashton glanced up and caught Zoe warring with herself.

"It's supposed to rain tonight," she said finally.

"Oh." His right hand was still resting on the doorknob.

"You could..." Her arms were crossed, her shoulders hunched. She glanced toward the guest room. "You should stay indoors in case it gets bad."

"Are you sure?" His grip on the doorknob tightened as Houdini appeared close by, his gray butt wiggling as he anticipated a longed-for escape.

"It wouldn't be right to leave you out in a storm." She stepped into her bedroom, gently swinging the door shut without a goodnight. The latch clicked into place and Ashton relaxed, letting go of the tension that had seeped into his body.

"Sorry, pal, no breakaway for you tonight," he said to the feline, who had pressed his nose into the crack between front door and jamb.

Ashton hesitated, then padded to the guest room. He'd been keeping his bags in his car, careful not to overstep. He should go out and get his toothbrush and pajamas. Instead, he stretched out on the made-up bed, face to the ceiling, Tiny curling against his side as Ashton pondered where his tentative friendship with Zoe might go next.

ZOE STOOD in the doorway in the morning, watching Ashton sleep. The storm hadn't materialized with the ferocity predicted by the weatherman, and she wondered what she was going to do with Ashton tonight. Let him stay? Kick him out again? He'd obviously needed a good night's sleep. He hadn't even changed out of his clothes, and was flat on his back, no blanket over him. It made her nurturing side want to care for him.

It didn't help that he was a paying guest of the resort, and she could lose her job if Dallas found out she was making Ashton stay out back.

Well, Ashton had volunteered. But still. It looked bad.

Maybe she could beg Vicky, and everyone else she knew, to let her stay with them. Except Vicky's landlord didn't allow pets, Margie from the front desk was allergic to cats, and Trent and his wife, Jenny, from housekeeping, had just had a baby. The friend list went on, as did the reasons not to crash with them.

Ashton's eyes flickered open, his mouth turning down in a frown. He blinked twice, then sat up. The tight lines that had grooved his cheeks relaxed when he spotted her, and a smile sneaked its way onto her face. Suddenly the whole day felt full of opportunity.

No. No hope. Just because last night had been nice, reminding her of better times, didn't mean she forgave him, or that she could afford to offer him any form of encouragement.

Their old relationship had been seriously flawed in a way she still didn't understand, and she couldn't let herself slip into old habits just because they were comfortable, and she still longed for them with a ferocity that scared her.

"Good morning." Ashton rubbed his face with the palm of his hand. "Wow. I don't even remember falling asleep."

"I guess a real bed helps."

"It's not bad in the tent," he said quickly.

"You know I'm strong enough to handle the truth."

"Maybe it's more about enduring judgment from the woman you love, because you know you failed her," he said, barely audibly, as he swung his legs over the side of the bed. He sat there for a while, unmoving, his gaze on the whitewashed wall in front of him.

He still loved her.

She let that sink in for a moment before saying, "Why do you think I'd judge you?"

He turned his head, holding her gaze, jaw tight. "Because I judge myself." He stood. "I'm going to work on your yard." He came closer, no doubt planning to push past and avoid further conversation. Zoe held her ground.

"Why…" Zoe paused, choosing her words carefully. "Why are you judging yourself?"

"Because," he said impatiently, "I was a nice guy who let myself get suckered into trying to do the right thing."

"Into caring for a child who wasn't yours? But how could you know? Your intentions were noble." Zoe knew his own father hadn't been around to raise him, and that stepping in must have been a no-brainer. But he'd been used, and those wounds still had to be raw. Still, she didn't think it was right that he was judging himself for the actions of others.

He didn't answer, his face tight with emotion.

"How long ago did your wife pass away?"

Ashton rubbed his face again. "Four months."

"What happened?"

"She was sick."

"Did you love her?"

"No. No, Zoe," he said softly, a hint of impatience still present, but also a great sorrow weighting his words. "I never loved her. And we weren't intimate, either. Not after I went back." He met Zoe's eyes, and she sucked in a breath at the depth of love she saw, because it was for her and her only.

He'd come here for forgiveness, but she could see that he first had to forgive himself. It made her heart ache in a brand-new way, to know that how things had ended had hurt him, too. She somehow found it difficult to blame him so deeply, for he felt like a victim of the situation as well.

Before she could think what to say, he brushed past her, his footsteps a staccato beat down the front steps. She suspected that if she looked out the window she would see him sprinting across the sandy beach, as though trying to outrun his own emotions and feelings of failure.

* * *

ASHTON PACED across Zoe's backyard, then frowned. He kept losing count. He turned, going back to the fence that separated her yard from the neighbor's, stirring up the dogs on the other side of the boards once again.

Woof, woof.

"Quiet, Archie. Quiet, Jughead," he called. The dogs

hushed temporarily, and he once again paced the few steps from the fence to where the gazebo would go.

One. Two. Three.

Was that too close to the property line? If it went here, then the shrub he'd been given by Caroline should go there, between the fence and future gazebo.

He moved to the fence to pace it out again.

Woof, woof.

"Quit teasing my dogs!" hollered a man from an upstairs window.

Ashton looked up, an apology on his lips.

"Ashton!" Bob called in surprise. "Mary said she thought it was you ripping apart Zoe's yard yesterday. I told her to get her eyes checked, but I'll be a monkey's uncle. It is you. Are you two back together again?"

"No, sir. Sorry I got the dogs bothered."

"They probably just want to say hello is all. They missed you tossing a ball for them down on the beach. With Mary's bum knee we don't make it out onto the uneven sand very often anymore. Are you in town to stay?"

"Until the end of November for sure."

"Must be filling in for Sandra over at the school then?"

Ashton nodded. "I am."

"And what are you doing to Zoe's yard?"

"Fulfilling a promise."

The man chuckled. "I don't think that's the one she'd been planning on you fulfilling. She just about had her place sold to my son before you left." He winked and pulled his head inside, closing the window.

Ashton focused on his pacing and counting again, but found he couldn't.

The promise she'd been planning on him fulfilling was marriage. Family. Everything he'd wanted with her, too.

It had to eat her up inside to know that he'd walked out

on her, to provide a family for someone else. And it ate him up to know that he'd blindly stepped in to do what the real father, Quentin, should have done. Instead, it was Ashton who'd sacrificed his life plans and personal preferences to be there when Maliki had been ill. It had been Ashton who'd found a way to cover Jaelyn's life-saving surgeries needed at birth. And for what? For Quentin to come swooping in a few weeks after Maliki's death and claiming the now healthy baby, depriving Ashton of the daughter he'd thought was truly his.

The anger and self-loathing that had plagued Ashton when he'd woken up that morning returned. What kind of man took a woman's hopes and dreams and squandered them on a liar who had only been using him? How had he not known?

He sat in the dewy grass and rested his head in his hands. Last August, faced with the dilemma of staying with Zoe or helping his unborn child and her ill mother, it had all made sense.

But now, after seeing everything for what it truly was, he wondered how he could ever begin to ask Zoe to forgive him.

CHAPTER 4

"He left you. He's still not telling you everything," Zoe muttered to herself. She placed her palms on the vanity and leaned toward the mirror, staring her reflection in the eye. Sighing, she picked up her flatiron and with a few deft moves taught by her hairdresser, used it to put soft curls in her hair.

She set down the iron and met her own eyes again. "You're going to forgive him, aren't you? He broke your heart once. Who's to say he won't again?"

She continued to argue with herself. "He regrets how things ended, and it's obviously caused him pain. Everyone deserves a second chance."

Despite everything, she felt whole when he was around, and she'd missed that. Having him back, she had to admit, was nice. Really nice.

The fact that he could barely forgive himself, and yet was here, trying, and still in love with her, too... He'd made a mistake and was attempting to make amends.

They both needed to heal, but maybe they could help each

other through it somehow. But to do that, she needed more answers.

Answers she was going to have to patiently pry out of him, by the looks of things.

It was so like Ashton to help someone even if it meant great personal sacrifice. So like him to blame himself if things didn't work out.

And it was also so like her to want to try and fix him, she thought with a sigh.

But maybe it was none of that. Maybe they were both simply seeking closure, for understanding, so they could move on. Apart.

She hoped not though. She hoped it was more than that.

Zoe unplugged the flatiron and checked the time. She fired off a text to Dallas, telling him she might be a few minutes late for work.

She hopped in her car and headed across town. A few minutes later she was walking around her house, to find Ashton sitting on the back lawn, head in his hands.

She wasn't sure if she should hurry over to see if he was all right, or pretend she hadn't seen him and scoot off to work. But before she could weigh her options, she found herself saying his name aloud.

He looked up.

"You okay?" she asked.

"Fine," he said briskly, getting up. "Just thinking." He seemed wary, the walls going up around him.

She reached for his arm so he wouldn't turn away or shut her out.

"You're not the only one who has to forgive themselves," she said in a rush.

His head snapped up in surprise. "What are you talking about? You did absolutely nothing wrong. Ever."

"Maybe I could have helped. I stepped back out of fear of smothering you, and maybe I shouldn't have."

"I didn't give you a chance to be there for me," he said hesitantly, and she wondered if he'd truly believed she hadn't cared when she'd stepped back, giving him space to deal with things last summer.

"But I didn't force the issue, either. I thought...I thought maybe we were moving too fast for you—"

"We weren't."

"And then I thought that maybe I'd spooked you into running straight into the arms of another."

"You didn't."

She swallowed. "I also thought that maybe our love wasn't as real as I'd believe it to be. That maybe you didn't love me as much as I loved you."

He squeezed a tape measure, looking as if he wanted to be anywhere but facing her right now. But instead of turning away, he spoke. "I wondered the same thing when you were so quiet about me leaving for the city, and then when I stretched out my stay. But I want you to know that my love for you will always be real."

Zoe nodded again, her throat thick because she'd felt the depth of his love, which was why her heartbreak had been so confusing, so crushing. There were some things you just couldn't lie about. Not when you felt it so deeply it became part of your personal truth.

"I have a coffee break at three," Zoe said quickly, before she lost her courage. "Will you join me?"

Ashton's eyes met hers, his hands suddenly still.

"If you bring me anything other than a cinnamon bun, though, I'll think it's a sign you aren't interested in seeing if we can become friends again."

His shoulders relaxed. "I'd like to be friends."

"I think I would, too." She shifted awkwardly, her heart

hurting from the effort of letting go of her pain so she could make room for the future and whatever it might bring.

* * *

ASHTON ZIPPED AROUND THE BACKYARD. He needed to dig just one more hole before he left to meet Zoe for her coffee break.

He couldn't be late. Zoe was offering him a lifeline.

She'd tried to take some of the blame for their breakup, but it wasn't hers to take.

He stopped moving. He needed to find the courage to tell her the whole truth. She was the kind of person who felt comfort in knowing everything, even the things he'd rather leave where they belonged—in the past.

He just hoped his failures didn't cause him to fall too deeply in her estimation.

Ashton finished the hole, and quickly leaned the shovel beside the small plastic garden shed he and Zoe had built from a kit last year, early on in their budding relationship. She'd had it delivered and had been staring at it in her front yard when he'd happened by on an evening walk. At that point they'd been out on only one date, even though they texted fairly regularly, and he'd ended up stopping to help her.

It had been a perfect evening where they'd laughed and talked, the time flying by. It was while putting the roof on the small unit that he'd realized he wanted to marry her. Her smile and willingness to bend instead of fight had won him over, as well as her contradictory quickness to stand firm and say her piece when she knew she was in the right.

And yet, when he'd left her for Maliki, she hadn't stood up for their relationship, but had remained silent. He understood now that it was because she'd been afraid of losing him. If he'd given her the chance to come forward and speak, would things have turned out differently?

He knew they would have. It was the reason he'd shut her out. She would have convinced him to help from afar rather than diving in like he had.

Realizing he'd spent the past five minutes staring at the shed, caught in the past, Ashton hightailed it over to Sweet Caroline's to pick up their afternoon treat.

He hustled up to the counter, where Caroline was starting a fresh pot of coffee.

"Ashton, go wash your hands."

He glanced down and caught sight of the fingerprints he'd left on her pristine counter.

"Yes, ma'am."

When he returned from cleaning up, he met her at the counter again.

"Two cinnamon buns to go, please."

She shook her head. "All sold out. Cookies? Pie?" She waved to the glass display filled with other goodies.

His hands went to the glass as Zoe's words replayed in his mind. *If you bring me anything other than a cinnamon bun, though, I'll think it's a sign you aren't interested in seeing if we can become friends again.*

It had to be cinnamon buns. He gave Caroline a desperate look. "Day olds? Week olds? Please. They have to be—"

"I'm all out, hon."

"Can you call Zoe and tell her that?"

"And why would I do that?" Caroline asked. Her eyebrows suddenly lifted as comprehension dawned. "Ah. I see." She moved to the pies, dishing out two slices of key lime into a takeout box. "She likes my pie."

"Can you call her? Please?"

Caroline nodded and wiped her hands on the gingham

apron tied around her waist. "Sure, dear." She lifted her chin to the man waiting in line behind Ashton.

He refused to give up his spot until she promised. "Please?"

"I said I would."

"Now?"

"As soon as I have a free moment. Now hurry along or her break will be over before you get there."

She shooed him away, and Ashton reluctantly left. When he reached the guest services desk it was already ten past three and Zoe was just finishing a conversation with a woman in baggy shorts, a dab of blue paint on her cheek.

"Ashton, this is Hope Ryan, my assistant."

"Pleased to meet you." Hope smiled, hefting a panel with a beach scene painted on it.

"She helps me with weddings. She's an artist, assistant…everything!"

"Speaking of weddings, I'd better get these hung before I head home." Hope and her painting disappeared out the lobby's side door.

"I'm sorry I'm late," Ashton said.

"Thanks for bringing us some buns," Zoe said, taking the container as she walked around her desk. Her hair had lost some of the curl it had had this morning, but it still bounced as she led him outside. "I was just finishing up the latest newsletter, and I'm hoping you can check it out later to see if I got the automation thing set up correctly. It's definitely more complicated than I thought it would be."

"Sure. Sweet Caroline's was—"

"I'm so glad you brought her cinnamon buns. They're my favorite." She turned, giving him a bright smile that made his heart stop. That smile was for him. Nobody else.

"She was out of—"

"This is just like old times. If even one thing was out of place it wouldn't be the same, would it?"

"Did Caroline call?" he asked nervously.

"Why?" They were outside now, at a picnic table in the shade, where a nice breeze came off the ocean. Perfect view, perfect temperature, perfect companion. There was only one problem.

Zoe sat at one end of the bench and looked up at him, a silent invitation for him to sit beside her. He sat, facing her the best he could.

"Caroline—" he began, but Zoe had opened the box, her ready smile fading. "They were all out. I asked Caroline to call and tell you that this isn't a sign I don't want to be friends. There's actually nothing I'd like more."

Zoe was trying to suppress a smile.

"What's so funny?"

"Caroline didn't need to call." She laughed, handing him one of the forks the café owner had placed inside the container. "Shall we?"

"You knew?"

She took a bite of the pie, her lips still curved upward in amusement. "I did."

"If we were closer to the ocean, I'd toss you in," he grumbled.

"I had you going, didn't I?"

"She never runs out of cinnamon buns. I thought you were going to…I don't know, but it wouldn't be good." He felt exhausted from the constant stress of worrying.

Zoe was smiling, her eyes lit up with mischief. "This is for the dirty rotten egg thing."

"How is this about that?" he muttered. "You were the one trying to cheat by going in without changing into your bathing suit."

She laughed and he got the feeling she was holding something back.

"What aren't you telling me?"

Zoe took another bite of pie, giving him a triumphant and slightly smug look. "I'm guessing Caroline sold out around seven this morning, because she had a large order come in from the resort, and then didn't have time to bake more because of a large cookie order. Which was also from the resort."

"You knew." He waved his fork at her. "You set me up."

She giggled and leaned away. An invitation. Ashton dropped his fork and reached for her, tickling her ribs. She shifted and squirmed, her body landing against his. She felt so good, so right. He slowed his onslaught, inhaling the scent of her hair.

He felt his whole world open up when he was with her. How had he ever believed it was right to leave her side even for one moment?

"I missed you."

Zoe glanced up at him from her spot against his chest before carefully putting space between them again. She smoothed her hair, avoiding his gaze as she said, "I missed you, too."

He was overcome with gratitude and hope. If only forgiving himself would come as naturally as being friends with Zoe.

* * *

ZOE FINISHED work and met Ashton outside. There was a five o'clock wedding happening on the beach, but in an uncharacteristic move, she'd left the details completely in the hands of the wedding coordinator—the bride's mother. The woman knew where everything was, and had Hope's number if she needed anything.

Over the past year, Zoe had become a zealot when it came to making sure every bride had her perfect day. But when Ashton mentioned renting a paddleboard from the resort that evening, she'd seized the moment to spend more time with him. Just to get to the bottom of his marital mystery, she told herself. Not to fill that void that had been achingly present since he'd left a year ago. The void that seemingly only one man could fill: Ashton.

The plan was to drive to a quiet cove just outside town where breakers wouldn't knock them around as they stood on the wide boards and tried to navigate the open water like Venetian gondoliers.

"As a resort guest I feel I should be paying to use the sports equipment. Are you sure it's okay to borrow these?" Ashton asked, as he strapped two paddleboards to the roof of his car.

"No, I became a huge rule breaker after you left me," Zoe teased.

A furrow appeared between Ashton brows and she quickly apologized for sinking a knife into the wound they were both trying to mend. "That wasn't fair."

"It's okay. I know you were joking." He met her gaze over the hood of his car. "Shall we?" He'd snugged the last strap, tucking its loose end deftly into place before opening the driver's side door.

Once they were seated she shifted to face him as he pulled out of the resort parking lot, determined not to let things get awkward. "Ashton—"

"It's fine. Really."

She didn't intend for him to sweep everything under the rug, or for her to give the impression that breaking her heart had been fine. But they were never going to move past things if they continued on the way they were.

At a stop sign Ashton looked over to give her a half smile, but she could see the strain. She reminded herself that in the last few months he'd lost not only his wife, but also the child he'd believed was his.

"It's okay to still be grieving," Zoe assured him. "It's natural."

"I didn't love her," he said with an unfamiliar stubbornness.

"But you married her. You're still going to grieve."

"I'm...*mad* at Maliki." The energy radiating off Ashton was impressive. He was squeezing the steering wheel and he let out a shaky breath. "I'm furious at her, as well as myself."

"According to psychologists, anger is one of the five stages of grief."

"It's not grief-induced. Trust me."

They were at the edge of town now, and Ashton stopped at a crosswalk for a family pushing a stroller. He was frowning at them, his gaze trailing after them as they made it safely from the parking lot across to the boardwalk and beach.

"Do you miss the baby, too?" Zoe asked softly.

For a moment she thought he was going to ignore the question, shut her out.

"Yeah." He nodded. "Like crazy."

"It must've been difficult to lose what you thought was going to be your family."

"Maliki wanted what was best for her baby," Ashton said, as he pulled out onto the highway that ran along the coast.

"But not for you?"

"Obviously," he said, his tone hard, unforgiving.

Sand drifted across the asphalt in one wind-swept spot, and Ashton said, "Are you sure this cove isn't going to be full of waves? I'm starting to think you're taking me out here to drown me. Or at least laugh at me before I do it myself."

"The wind is coming from the right direction. The cove will be perfect, I promise."

At a solitary palm tree and an old, faded wood sign, Zoe directed Ashton to turn right. He parked the car in the secluded paved lot and they looked out over the quiet water.

"Told ya it would be calm." Zoe pointed to the hills sheltering the cove. "This all blocks the prevailing wind."

They put on their life preservers and carried the paddles to the shore, returning to retrieve the long boards. "I got some really nice feedback on today's newsletter," she said.

"Yeah?"

"Yeah. Thanks for your help."

"I didn't do much, but you're welcome."

Since his night inside the cottage, he hadn't gone back to the tent. And Zoe had stopped looking for a place to move to, knowing her own home would soon be ready for her and the cats, and that their current roommate situation would be fine until then.

They spent an hour out on the water, Ashton picking up the sport with ease. Finally tired from paddling, Zoe sat down on her board, hugging her legs as she watched him navigate about. He had a serious look that almost gave him a childlike innocence.

Noticing that she was taking a break, Ashton paddled her way, then sat down and let his board drift against hers.

"You know what I could go for?" Zoe asked.

"What?"

"S'mores." Melted chocolate and marshmallow smushed between two graham crackers. Yum. "Whoever invented them should have gotten an award."

"Do they still make them on the beach every night?"

"Guests can with the group, but I happen to know

someone who has a key to the cupboard where everything is kept. She also knows about a private fire pit a little ways from the resort."

"I happen to like that person." Ashton's warm, crooked smile made her heart lift.

"I'll have to remember that."

They drifted for a while, watching a pod of porpoises across the cove, playing or fishing, she wasn't sure which.

"Ashton?" Zoe asked, breaking the silence. "Why didn't you fight for the baby?"

"She wasn't rightfully mine."

"But you were…" She cleared the sudden emotion from her throat. "You were married to her mother, and she used you—wanted you to be the dad by, the sound of it. Doesn't that count for something?"

"I thought it did. I was listed on the birth certificate, and Maliki said Jaelyn was mine. But two weeks after Maliki passed on Quentin appeared, insisting that she was his. I took him to court. Maliki knew I wasn't the father. She lied to me and used me, because Quentin had told her he didn't want to be a dad and wouldn't help her."

"Surely the courts took that into account?"

"Quentin claimed he didn't know about Jaelyn until after Maliki died. He was adamant, and the court mandated paternity tests even though the math put Jaelyn as mine, not his." He winced as if retelling the story physically hurt. "I felt self-righteous about him being in the wrong, up until the crushing moment of truth. Maliki had lied to me, used me and even cheated on me. Jaelyn wasn't mine, and the courts agreed she should be with Quentin."

Ashton fell quiet, his face a mask of anger, betrayal and pain.

Horrified on his behalf, Zoe stared out over the water for a moment. To step out of a good relationship to marry a woman you thought was carrying your child. Then to have her pass away, and the real father step forward and take away the baby you thought was yours... What a slap across the face.

"That's awful." No wonder he didn't want to talk about it.

"I still don't know why he changed his mind about wanting her. They did home studies, the works, and deemed him—a man with a criminal past—to be adequate father material. I've spent the past three and a half months..." His voice gave out and he took a moment to collect himself as Zoe reached over to squeeze his hand in silent support. "I've had to help him build a relationship with Jaelyn so he can be her dad. And every time I had to say goodbye..." His voice broke again, the anguish he was trying to disguise, so deep it brought tears to Zoe's eyes.

"I'm so sorry, Ashton."

He shook his head briskly. "It's over now. She's his. I have no further responsibilities."

Zoe wished she could say the right thing—whatever would remove the pain from his tortured gaze.

She just didn't know what it was.

* * *

ASHTON LEANED BACK against the log resting in the sand, a piece of driftwood polished by the ocean waves. After paddleboarding, Zoe had led him past the resort fire pit, where guests were swapping tales and roasting marshmallows. They'd kept walking with their pilfered supplies and blanket, until they were at what amounted to a private beach, secluded and quiet, and beautifully tranquil as the sun dipped below the horizon.

They'd built a fire together, using smaller pieces of

driftwood that had collected along the edge of the grassy dunes during a storm.

"Want this one?" Ashton asked, angling the roasting stick with a toasted marshmallow in Zoe's direction. She had settled into the sand beside him, not quite touching, but close enough that he could feel her warmth and the brush of her shirtsleeve whenever she moved.

She plucked the browned marshmallow off the stick and jammed it between two cookies and a square of chocolate, making a sandwich. She didn't wait for the chocolate to melt before taking a bite.

"Mmm," she said. "My favorite."

Ashton reached for another marshmallow and began toasting it for himself.

Between battling the waves on the paddleboard and working hard in Zoe's yard, he was comfortably tired. Add in the emotional drain of reiterating part of his Maliki and Quentin story and he was bordering on exhausted. It didn't help that the crackling fire, empty beach and relaxing sound of the waves, as well as Zoe's warmth beside him, were soothing.

He finished making his last s'more and dug a little deeper into the sand so he could use the log for a pillow, relaxing as he savored his snack.

The careful wall Zoe had maintained when he'd first arrived had been steadily dissolving and they were coming close to their old pattern of friendship. Things were still strained and awkward at times, but he had hope for tomorrow, as well as hope that Zoe would be there with him.

He licked melted marshmallow off his fingers and brushed the crumbs from his shirt. Zoe imitated his pose in the sand, but curled onto her side so she faced him. Ashton twisted to inhale the scent of her hair again.

"You smell like sunshine, the ocean and the sweetness of toasted sugar."

"It's a special scent only available in Indigo Bay." She wiped at something stuck to his chin. "What are you going to do after the maternity leave is done?"

"I suppose it depends where things are by then. I missed the community and kids when I was away. It's different in the city."

The firelight was dancing, making her eyes gleam as she glanced up at him.

"I was thinking," he added, "that maybe I'd try and find something more permanent than the cottage." Stay awhile. A long while.

Zoe was silent, but he didn't take it as something to fear, as they'd always given each other time to consider things, even mid-conversation.

"I still don't understand why you left without telling me everything," she said.

Ashton's heart rate increased, and he fought the instinct to clam up. He needed to tell Zoe everything, but he feared he was going to only add to the pain he saw in her eyes, that he was going to drive her even further away.

He shifted to a sitting position and cleared his throat, reminding himself that he could tell Zoe everything—in fact, he needed to if he ever wanted to have a true second chance with her.

"I deserve the truth."

"I know. But the truth hurts."

"Not knowing the truth hurts, too."

"I was trying to protect you."

"How?"

"From what I was doing. And from the hurt. It feels foolish now, but at the time…" His words caught in his throat. "But at the time I started to believe that what we had couldn't possibly be real. And when you became distant and weren't pushing me to talk about it, it felt like proof."

She leaned away from him, and he quickly added, "It wasn't your fault. I know now that you were trying to give me space. I was kidding myself, using your behavior as an excuse to validate what I was doing because it wasn't all on the up-and-up." He thought of the way he'd married Maliki to save on medical bills. "I was being selfish, and was looking for anything to make me feel better about leaving you, anything to keep me in the city so I would do what I thought was the right thing instead of running back to you."

She'd paused, no longer looking like she wanted to storm off.

"What do you mean, 'on the up-and-up'?"

"I married Maliki so she would be covered for medical expenses. She was very sick."

He waited, giving Zoe a moment to absorb that fact. She didn't look quite as stunned as he'd expected.

"A marriage of convenience? Insurance fraud?" she asked.

"That's why I couldn't tell you."

"You thought I'd rat you out?" She was ticked now, her cheeks flushing.

"No, but well, maybe. I don't know. It didn't feel like fraud, but I could see how it could be painted that way and my head was all over the place. I thought I was going to lose Jaelyn before she was even born, and the only way to truly help was to step all the way in. But I didn't marry Maliki because I loved her," he added quickly.

Zoe's chest expanded and the hurt and anger in her eyes settled.

"Jaelyn was delivered by C-section a month early due to Maliki's declining health, as well as her own. Jaelyn had four surgeries before she was two months old. My health coverage paid for most of them as well as some of Maliki's expenses."

Ashton could feel the same rush of fear that he had during Jaleyn's birth. He could smell the hospital's soap on his skin, feel the heavy press of worry when she'd been rushed to the operating room straight from the delivery room. So small and precious, a life in peril.

He hadn't known whether to follow her on the gurney or to stay with Maliki. She'd been scared, too. For her baby, for her own health, and how she'd been weakened from the treacherous pregnancy.

In the end, he'd gone to Jaelyn as the nurses took care of her mother. He hadn't been able to be in the operating room during the procedure, obviously, and so had gone back to the maternity ward. For days he'd moved like a zombie between the maternity wing and the neonatal intensive care unit, trying to remain chipper and optimistic.

All he'd wanted was to call Zoe, let her know how much he missed her, to hear her voice telling him it was all going to be okay.

Instead, he'd toughed it out, snapping at parking lot attendants for a scratch on his old car, and at clowns for trying to make him smile while he passed through the hospital lobby.

He'd never liked clowns.

Maliki had been released, then Jaelyn. Maliki had never recovered fully, her health moving in the opposite direction of their growing daughter's.

"Is Jaelyn okay now?" Zoe asked.

Ashton blinked, his mind returning from the past.

"I'm sorry, what?" he asked.

"The surgeries? They went okay?"

"Yeah, all of them went really well and things are fine."

He wanted to say more, to spill every little detail, but he found himself suddenly exhausted.

"I let you down," he said to Zoe. "It hurt to give our future to someone else, and I know that stepping up and taking ownership of the situation was the right thing to do for Jaelyn because she got world-class medical care that she might not have otherwise. But I still regret it, every single moment, because it kept us apart. It kept me from being with you, and I wish I had found a better way to resolve things."

Zoe stared at him for one long, life-changing moment before, teary-eyed, she rolled up onto her knees and gently placed a kiss against his forehead, with a sadness so deep it made his heart hurt in an all new way.

* * *

ZOE LAY in the sand next to Ashton, her head resting tentatively on his chest, the blanket she'd brought along folded over them, as she told him the story of a bride who'd damaged her dress the day of her wedding back in February. Ginger had sent an identical gown across the continent in record time, delaying the wedding by only thirty minutes. Thirty minutes that Zoe had spent sweating and handing out slices of cinnamon buns to the wedding guests.

In the end everything had worked out fine for the bride and groom, and Ashton had laughed in all the right places during Zoe's retelling.

"I'm tempted to give up my post at guest services and become a wedding coordinator," she admitted.

"You'd be good at it, but what would all those guests do without you at your desk?"

"Get married," she said with a laugh, shifting her head back to the log, as it felt too intimate to rest against him in what was essentially a snuggle.

She finally felt as though Ashton was letting her in, increasing her understanding of why he'd left the way he had. It wasn't so much that he hadn't trusted her with the truth, or that they'd been moving too fast. It was more that he knew she would have talked him out of doing what he'd believed was the right thing. But she still didn't get why he'd felt the need to marry Maliki. It wasn't as though it was the 1940s, where single moms were looked down upon. He could have shared everything with Zoe and still been there as a father—something she knew was incredibly important to him.

He'd mentioned in passing that Maliki had been sick and in need—and had recently passed away. Had Ashton married her to provide medical insurance? If so, that had to have been an impossible choice, and Zoe could almost understand why he'd have to shut off his own life and step into Maliki's and the baby's.

Zoe still wished he would have talked to her, though. That was what couples who really loved each other did. It was what continued to keep her parents' marriage so strong, and it was what she and Ashton had failed at.

"Do you think you'll plan your own wedding?" Ashton asked, interrupting her thoughts.

The familiar sting came, as always, whenever anyone asked her whether she'd have her own special day. But this time it hurt even more because she knew Ashton was looking for a home here in Indigo Bay—one without her in it. He was asking about a wedding, but not assuming he'd be the groom.

And yet if he'd presumed to place himself in the picture, she'd be bothered.

"Of course," she said lightly. "Think you'll get remarried?"

"I hope to. I'd like to share my life with someone." His voice was sleepy, the stars above them as bright as if they were close enough to reach. "But I'm not sharing my half of the pineapple-free pepperoni pizza."

Zoe froze. What was he getting at? That he wanted a real, honest second chance with her? Not just forgiveness, but a true happily ever after?

"I'd share anything with you," he said, "but if you order pineapple, you're eating it."

Zoe smiled. "But pepperoni and pineapple are good together."

In the light from the dying fire she saw him pull a face. He looked over, meeting her gaze, and her heart thrummed. It felt like they were dancing around the idea of a relationship again. But it was difficult to let go of the fear, because nobody ever planned to break someone else's heart.

CHAPTER 5

T hey had spent the entire night out on the beach, talking and finding ways to push their painful past from the forefront of their minds.

It felt right. Like it always did with Zoe.

And this time Ashton wouldn't lose her. This time it was going to work. For the first time since arriving back in Indigo Bay he felt optimistic, and as though anything was possible.

Hooking his hand in Zoe's, he helped her up from the sand in the early dawn, then spun her around to dust her butt, causing her to jump.

"Ashton!" she scolded with a laugh.

"Sand."

She reached around him to smack his backside, but he beat her to it, taking care of the task himself.

"You don't trust me," she teased.

"I started something, and I'm certain you will quite happily finish it for me."

"You know me so well." She fell into step beside him, an arm wrapped companionably around his waist, the bag of leftover s'more supplies hanging from her free hand along with the blanket that had kept them warm as the chill settled in during the night.

"Let me take that for you," he said.

"I have it." She let him take it, anyway.

"I can't remember the last time I stayed out all night. That was really nice."

"We'll have to do it more often."

"But I know we probably won't."

She laughed. "Just because we never went back to play mini golf again even though we enjoyed it."

"Or ventured back to that bed-and-breakfast down the coast."

"We should go again."

"And eat sushi."

"We could skip the sushi." She was kicking sand as she walked, creating a spray in front of her.

"I thought you liked the cucumber roll."

"I did, but I don't miss it." She stopped moving, causing him to stop as well. She looked up at him, her face relaxed and sleepy despite the seriousness of her gaze. "I missed this."

"So did I." He lowered his lips to hers, kissing her as if they had all the time in the world and she rolled up onto her toes to bring the kiss deeper. "Good thing you don't have to work today," he said as they broke apart.

"Breakfast at Sweet Caroline's?" she suggested.

A jogger ran by, giving them a wave as the sun rose higher in the sky, chasing away the last of the night's chill.

"Coffee would be awesome right about now," Ashton admitted.

"Scrambled eggs."

"Her homemade hash browns."

"Cinnamon buns. Fresh from the oven."

Before long their steps were lengthening as they hustled toward the promise of food.

* * *

ZOE PUSHED BACK from the table. "All that food made me sleepy."

"As well as staying up all night. You should get some rest."

"You should, too."

Ashton checked the clock on the café wall. "I have to accept a delivery in an hour."

"A delivery?"

"At your place. Yard stuff."

"I don't like the idea of you spending a ton."

"Why?"

"Because it's your money. And you should be saving up for other things." What they had right now between them felt nice, but it was still very tentative. If things didn't work out, she didn't want her yard to become his cross to bear, or a reminder to her of fresh pain.

"I'll worry about my money, honey." He stood, then leaned down to place a kiss on her forehead.

She ducked her head. The kiss earlier had been unexpected and nice, but she wasn't ready to be a couple.

"And anyway, the Realtor we texted on the beach has already gotten back to me about a fixer-upper I'm going to check out later."

Zoe toyed with the necklace that had been hidden under her shirt. "You're serious about staying?"

"Indigo Bay has always felt like home, and I like the people here."

"Oh, do you?" she said flirtatiously, despite the apprehension fluttering in her stomach.

The skin around his eyes crinkled as he smiled. "I do."

He was going to make her swoon if he kept that up, that was for certain. She wanted to stand up and kiss him, and she could easily see herself back in a relationship with him after the cozy opening up to each other on the beach last night.

But they were heading down the path of moving too fast, which meant she needed to slow it down, since whenever she rushed into a relationship it seemed to collapse. It was like her mother said, "If it's good, taking a little time won't make a world of difference."

The expression had never made much sense to Zoe, but her mom had managed to remain married for forty-three years. That was forty-three more than Zoe had accomplished.

"Good luck with the place," she said. "I need to head home and feed my cats. They're going to be mad at me for their late breakfast."

Ashton paid for their meals and headed out, while Zoe stayed to finish her cup of coffee. The cats could wait another minute or two while she mentally sorted out how quickly she'd gotten close to Ashton once again. He was opening up to her despite the obvious way it hurt him to do so. That was promising, wasn't it?

"Well?" Caroline asked, sliding into the seat across from her. "How are things?"

Zoe pondered the question for a moment before saying, "Do you believe in second chances?"

"Of course."

"Or is it naive of me to think that things might be different a second time?"

"I see the way you two look at each other. Whatever you've got, it's not common." She caught Zoe's expression. "It's a good thing. I was slack-jawed when I heard you two split up, you know."

"So was I." Zoe wrapped her hands around the cup. She hadn't seen it coming and didn't want to be blindsided again.

"Did he explain?"

She nodded.

"To your satisfaction?" Caroline asked, as though sensing Zoe's hesitation.

"Well, I want every tiny little detail." She'd always believed she tended to smother men, sending them running. But Ashton had admitted to shutting her out, as he'd expected her to smother him into changing his mind about doing the right thing. By not doing so, she'd let him go. The exact opposite of her ex-fiancé, Kurtis.

She just couldn't get it right, could she?

"Honey, I think that's called caring." Caroline cupped Zoe's hands, the mug in the middle. "Smothering is when you don't let up and are on a man twenty-four/seven, wanting to hear about every emotion flitting through his heart. You care, is all."

"Is that what it is? Because it feels like I never get it right. How much is too much? How much is not enough?" She looked down at her cup again. "Oh, I don't know."

"It's hard to know what the right thing is." Caroline pushed herself out of her chair. "That's why I recommend you follow your heart."

"That's what I did the first time."

"Don't give me that forlorn look. Haven't you spent the entire year moping around this beautiful little town, wishing things could be different? That he'd come back and you'd get a second chance?"

Zoe's spine straightened. "I didn't mope. And I didn't—"

"You didn't have to say a thing. It was written all over that pretty face of yours." Caroline patted Zoe's cheek. "Follow your heart, my dear. It'll be worth it."

"But what if—"

"Which 'what if' would you rather live with? Option one: What if the relationship doesn't last? Option two: What if I had only given him another chance?"

Zoe contemplated her mug. "I'm afraid if it doesn't work out again, I won't survive."

Caroline clucked and shook her head. "I don't think I've heard anything quite so dramatic in my whole entire life."

Zoe laughed, swiping at her tears.

"Now, get out there and live," her friend urged. "Life's half over. What are you going to make of what's left?"

"That's depressing." Zoe stood and faced the door. She didn't want to live with regrets. She didn't want a relationship what-if haunting her. "But bracing in all the right ways."

"The best cinnamon buns and the best advice. That's what keeps 'em coming back!" called Caroline as Zoe hit the street with a smile. She realized that she quite possibly, once again, was considering the only man she'd ever deeply loved, Ashton Wallace.

* * *

A FEW EVENINGS after their all-nighter on the beach, Ashton covered Zoe's eyes and walked her the last few feet toward her house. The insurance work would be complete by about week's end, the place finally livable once more. But it was the yard he wanted her to see.

"Can I look?" she asked. "I'm afraid I'm going to trip."

"I've got you." Her cool, smooth fingers were wrapped around his wrists as he guided her to the front walk. Her lashes tickled his palms as he lowered his hands.

"Surprise," he said.

She looked to her left, taking in the new camellia hedge. It would flower later in the year in a riot of gorgeous pink blooms, brightening an area that had once been spotty and dull. At their feet, where the public sidewalk met her private one, he'd replaced the old cracked concrete slabs with flat stones, beach sand tamped between them to help keep them in place.

She tipped her head up, taking in her white, blue-trimmed little Cape Cod-style cottage. "It's nice."

He took her hand, leading her onto the grass and around the side of the house. "There's more."

As they rounded the corner she gasped, her steps halting. She turned to him, eyes ablaze with delight. "Ashton!"

She hurried forward, clasping a hand over her mouth as she took in what he felt was the best part of the entire design—the gazebo he'd promised not to get for her. But Dallas knew a guy who didn't want his anymore, and for a few hundred dollars in moving charges, the large cedar structure was now looking splendid in Zoe's yard. He'd strung the gables with patio lanterns and hung strands of fairy lights above the eating area. He'd partially enclosed the sides with a gauzy fabric recommended by the florist when he'd picked up a small bouquet as a centerpiece.

The table in the gazebo was set for two.

"This is amazing." She turned to him and planted her free hand on his chest. "Thank you."

"You're welcome."

"But I thought we'd settled on no gazebo."

"Dallas knew someone who was looking to have his relocated."

She turned to the structure again, leaning back against Ashton's chest. He took the hint and wrapped his arms around her, holding her close. "I don't even know how to express how amazing this is." She let out a squeal. "Is that a hammock?"

In the corner of the yard, where the side and back fences

met, he'd hung a sunny yellow one. Strategically placed bushes and flowerbeds gave it a private-escape feel.

"This must have been so expensive." She had slipped from his embrace and was taking in the details, her face lit with awe.

"When people heard I was doing your yard they all had something for you."

"Really?"

"This shrub is from Caroline. You know about the gazebo, and Dallas coordinating the move. The hammock is from the neighbors. The flowers from Miss Lucille."

"Her precious bluestars? You're joking?"

"Not her prize-winning ones. These were rejects she was planning to toss, but figured they were good enough for your yard."

"Oh, yes. Of course." Zoe nodded seriously.

"She made me promise that you wouldn't turn them around and beat her out in the annual competition."

"That almost makes me want to develop a green thumb."

Ashton pointed out a few more donated items, continuing the tour.

"This is amazing," she said, when he was done.

"Everyone wanted to be a part of something that made you smile."

"That's so sweet. Thank you. It's beautiful."

"Will you join me for supper?" he asked, drawing her toward the gazebo where a fresh crab salad was waiting on ice in a cooler.

"Tonight and every night," she said under her breath, following him.

And that was all he needed to know.

* * *

ZOE WATCHED Ashton over the rim of her wineglass. She was still stunned at the beauty of her yard, front and back. The gazebo was amazing, and the personal touches he'd added made it special. Made it hers. From the lights that hung above, to the literary quotes hanging on faux weathered boards, it was all perfect. And enjoying a meal with Ashton, here in the midst of it all, made it even better.

This was the man she knew and understood.

"This is so amazing," she repeated. "Thank you!"

Ashton smiled, feeling as though they were moving toward the right track. The one where he'd wake up happy for the rest of his life, her at his side, nuzzling in for a sweet, good-morning kiss.

"Hey, I haven't had a chance to ask—did you make an offer on the fixer-upper?" she asked.

His appointment to view the property had been pushed back to yesterday. He'd texted her saying the place had potential, and that he was seriously considering making an offer contingent on what an inspector said.

"It's structurally sound, and the areas that need work are things I already identified on my own, so that's reassuring. It's a big project, though."

"Will you live there while you renovate?"

"Probably."

"So you're buying it?"

He turned her hand over in his. "I can see you thinking."

"And what am I thinking?"

"That I don't have a contract with the school district beyond November."

She nodded. It was true. But she did love that he was looking at putting down roots, making plans to stick around.

"What if you can't find work locally after that?"

"I have other skills."

"You wouldn't be pursuing your passion."

"Maybe I have other passions." His sly smile warmed her gut, and made her want to giggle.

Stay focused, she chided herself. They were sliding in fast toward home plate, just like last time, and their relationship hadn't been strong enough to allow them to trust each other when things got tough. If she was going to let herself go down this path, she had to be sure they took things slower, and developed that trust.

She felt as though they were working on getting there, but hadn't quite arrived. Hadn't quite dissected why things had gone wrong last time.

"If I decide I don't want to live there," Ashton said, "I can sell it for a profit or rent it out when the renovations and updates are complete."

"So either way you can't lose?"

"There's always a way to lose," he said, with a meaningful glance.

She took the last sip of her wine.

"More?" he asked, letting go of her hand and lifting the bottle.

"No, thanks."

They sat for a moment, letting the conversation sink in.

He was staying in Indigo Bay. Was he staying for her?

"I was wondering, would you want to play mini golf next weekend?" Ashton asked.

"Mini golf?" She set down her glass.

"Maybe stay at a bed-and-breakfast."

Like old times.

"As friends?" she asked pointedly.

"Of course."

They finished their dessert, a decadent chocolate mousse, in awkward silence. When Zoe heard her phone ringing deep inside her purse, which she'd ditched at the entrance to the gazebo, she just about flung herself at it.

Her heart had wanted him to say "more than friends," but she was also relieved he hadn't.

"Sorry," she said to Ashton, as she lifted the phone to her ear.

"Zoe, it's Dallas."

"Is everything all right?" She didn't want to leave, but didn't want to stay, either. She was afraid of what her next reaction might be. It could be anything from take Ashton to bed to fight with him.

They had reached a tentative forgiveness, and it scared her. She wanted the future, but didn't want to repeat their past mistakes, and those still felt inevitable.

"I've been meaning to ask about that tent I saw pitched behind your cottage a few nights back."

"There's no tent." Hadn't been for almost a week now.

"Oh?" Dallas asked, a hint of amusement tingeing his voice. "Where are you staying?"

"My house'll be done in a few days. And don't leap to conclusions," she said in a hushed voice as she padded across the lawn. Ashton must have been watering it, for it felt plush and wonderful underfoot. Amazing what a bit of dedicated care could do for it. "It's a two-bedroom cottage."

"That you're making Ashton pay for?" He quickly changed topics. "Speaking of which, how's the newsletter coming?"

"He's been helpful. Maybe you could reimburse him the cost of the cottage?"

"He's your guest then?"

"Well, no."

"So it's complicated?" She could hear the teasing tone in Dallas's voice.

Zoe glanced over her shoulder. Ashton was sitting patiently, waiting for her. "Not yet."

"Speaking of Ashton, the real reason I'm calling is because

there was someone here looking for him. There's a message at the front desk. But I wasn't sure where to find him, since his tent was gone, and nobody was answering the door or phone at the cottage."

Zoe ignored the implied innuendo. "He's showing me what he did to my yard. Do you want me to put him on the phone so you can pass on the message?"

"Sure. How do you like the gazebo?"

"I love it," Zoe declared, as she made her way back to Ashton. The structure, complete with the lights and gauzy curtains, looked romantic and dreamy in the fading evening sun. She could only image what it would be like once the climbing roses he'd planted around the base began to soften it. "Thanks for helping him get it here."

"He wants to impress you."

"I know."

"Is it working?"

"Time will tell."

She smiled and handed the phone to Ashton, then tried not to eavesdrop, especially when she could tell by Ashton's expression that the message was an important one.

* * *

"WHO'S LOOKING FOR YOU?" Zoe was watching him, and Ashton felt as though he was being tested, to see whether he'd open up about the call.

"Quentin. Jaelyn's real dad."

"What does he want?"

"I don't know."

Zoe was eyeing him closely, analyzing everything he didn't say. He knew the yard, the romantic dinner, followed by the promise of a trip, had been him pushing things a bit fast. She was already on edge, and he feared this small thing could easily become a fight.

"Are you going to call him back?" she asked.

"I don't know. After my last court-mandated visit to ensure Jaelyn was completely settled in, he made it very clear he didn't want me in their lives." Ashton was sitting at the table, and he poured himself another glass of wine, wishing it was something stronger.

"But aren't you curious why he's trying to find you?" She took the seat across from him, her brow creased in concern. "Or worried?"

"Curious, yes. Worried? Trying really hard not to be." Ashton was struggling to remain as cool and calm as he wanted to be. Quentin had cleaned up his life before claiming his daughter, but Ashton was still nervous for her, despite the court's home visits and investigations proving that he was a fit father. But after Maliki died, a few unsavory people had come by the apartment looking for Quentin, and Ashton worried that maybe his past was catching up with him.

Or, more likely, Quentin was already missing the free babysitting provided by Ashton. Otherwise known as his court-appointed visits to help transition Jaelyn into her new home.

"Jaelyn's in state-approved hands," Ashton said, unsure whether he was trying to ease the worry pinching Zoe's lips, or his own.

"You should call him."

"Yeah." He was afraid what he might say to the man. Afraid what he might hear.

"For Jaelyn," she urged.

He closed his eyes. It hurt being dragged back into Quentin's business, Jaelyn's life.

Quentin had rejected Maliki and Jaelyn when she'd

approached him in her first trimester. So Maliki had decided to go it alone until her prognosis—a bad one—had come in. Then she'd looked up Ashton. Things hadn't turned out anywhere close to the way she'd planned, and while he'd fought hard for Jaelyn, at the end of the day she simply wasn't his, and Quentin had proved to be a fit father.

It left a serious knot in Ashton's stomach when he thought about how the man who'd rejected Jaelyn was now raising her, as it had been Ashton sitting by her crib in the neonatal intensive care unit for days on end, fretting over every surgery. He felt as if he'd given up everything for Maliki and Jaelyn. And now what did he have left? A hurt and skittish Zoe, who he still loved with all his heart, and a lost daughter, plus medical debt the courts wouldn't transfer to Quentin.

But Ashton believed in second chances. He had to. He was counting on one himself.

CHAPTER 6

Ashton had tried calling Quentin, but the man didn't pick up, and didn't reply to his messages. Ashton tried not to assume the worst. He had his overnight trip with Zoe to focus on instead, and he liked how they were settling into new routines, a new friendship.

She'd insisted on driving, which he figured was her way of maintaining a semblance of control.

"Where do you see yourself in a year? Five years?" Zoe asked, as she slowed to take an exit off the divided highway.

It was an old game of theirs, where they'd present silly answers in an attempt to make the other laugh. But he knew Zoe was trying to get at something more than that today.

Ashton exhaled slowly, focusing on what to say. The problem was, he wanted to tell her exactly where he saw himself: married to her. In five years they'd have three adopted children running around in the backyard of a not-yet-paid-for larger home, the two of them cuddled in a hammock, watching their kids, hearts warm and full.

Happiness. Contentment. Fulfillment. Family.

And he was fairly certain that would spook her at this

point, as he'd seen the wariness in her eyes when he'd mentioned buying a place in town. But he also didn't want her to think he was feeling cavalier, or taking her extended olive branch for granted.

"Ashton?" she prompted.

"Five years. Living on a boat and battling scurvy."

"Aye, ye scurvy dog. Walk the plank!" she growled.

He chuckled. "And you?"

"Same as ever," she said with a theatrical sigh. "Dealing with yet another Oscar win."

"Then maybe in five years I see myself beating the paparazzi from your door. Pumping iron so I can be your devoted bodyguard."

"Oh, I like that idea. Carry me away from the crowds, big man."

"Your wish is my command."

They smiled, silence sifting back into the vehicle as palm trees and suburbs gave way to desolate sand dunes, before becoming beachside homes once again as they got closer to their destination.

"Do you really see yourself at my side in five years?" she asked.

And there it was.

"If you'll have me, yes. That's where I'd like to be."

"What would make me say no?"

"Say no?" He mentally stumbled, confused.

"Yeah."

"I don't pretend to know your mind," he said at last, "but I'll do whatever I can to prevent you from turning me away."

"I'm afraid we're going to repeat past mistakes," she blurted out. "That our relationship won't be strong enough."

"Okay," he said carefully.

She pushed her hair from her face. "Last time, we moved really fast and we didn't have the skills to overcome…life."

"So I guess I should have left the engagement ring back at the cottage, huh?"

She spared him a glance, not impressed with his joke.

"I'm just teasing. We're not going to let our past mistakes reoccur. I promise." There was no way he was being suckered again. Ever. Nothing could chase him away from Zoe. Unless it was her wish.

She slowed at an intersection outside a small town. "Is this where I turn? We got it wrong last time, but I can't remember if this was the way or not."

And wasn't that the metaphor for all her worries? Were they doing things right this time, or inadvertently repeating the past?

"Go left," he said decisively.

* * *

SINCE THE NIGHT of their supper in the gazebo, Zoe had been trying to figure out where she'd heard the unusual name Quentin before. As she pulled into the parking lot in front of the bed-and-breakfast, it came to her. The guy with the scar who kept coming into the resort had been asking for a Quentin. Quentin Valant. Was that Ashton's Quentin? And if so, who was the guy with the scar? And why did he want Quentin, who in turn was looking to speak with Ashton?

She mulled over why the whole thing felt off as she put the car in Park outside the bed-and-breakfast Hole-Inn-One. It was a little after noon, the day overcast but warm, and she put down her window as she turned off the car.

"Ashton?"

"Yeah?"

"Is Jaelyn's dad's last name Valant?"

"Yes. Why?" Ashton's stared out the windshield at the bird

feeder hanging off an oversize golf club in front of the sprawling B & B.

"Someone keeps coming by my desk at the resort asking if there's a reservation for Quentin Valant."

"Who is it?"

"I don't think he's ever left a name."

Ashton ran his hands down his thighs, his brow furrowed.

"What do you think's going on?" she asked.

"I don't know, but maybe I can find out. Quentin knows where I'm staying. Perhaps he told someone he was coming for a visit? It doesn't feel likely, but maybe." He lifted his phone and dialed a number, then left a message for Quentin, asking him to call back.

"What are we going to do?" Zoe asked when he was done.

The sat in silence for a long moment. "Mini golf?"

Zoe laughed. She supposed there really wasn't a ton they could do at the moment if Quentin wasn't answering his phone.

"Okay." She turned to him. "Thanks."

"For what?"

"For phoning him."

"Hopefully, when he returns my call it will be a socially acceptable time of day to drown my sorrows or rage." His faint smile was tinged with frustration.

"Oh, hon." She reached over to cup his cheek. "You know getting tipsy at lunchtime on Saturday in the South is just fine."

He acknowledged that with a twist of his lips. "Talking to him doesn't always bring out the best in me. I really resent how he claimed Jaelyn." Ashton heaved a sigh. "I'm desperate to see her, but I know it's better for her in the long run if I stay away." He shook his head, his heartbreak evident. "He said she was fine if I wasn't around."

"I'm sorry."

"Me, too." Zoe could see he was struggling to find the bright side. "I'm glad I was there when Jaelyn needed me, though. She's healthy now, because of it."

"Is that why Quentin refused to be named as the father? He knew she'd have big medical expenses?"

Ashton shook his head. "I don't think so. But I really don't know why he had a change of heart and came back for her. At least not the true reasons. I only know he wasn't there when Maliki and Jaelyn needed him."

Zoe gave his knee a squeeze. "But you were."

"Yeah."

But it meant losing Zoe, didn't it? What an impossible choice. She leaned over the gap between their seats and gave Ashton a long, slow kiss. He was such a good man.

"Let's go play golf," she whispered.

They climbed out of the car and took the two-minute walk to the zoo-themed course. It was next door to a real golf course that had a great clubhouse restaurant with a shrimp salad worth returning for.

They played the first four holes with Zoe slightly in the lead, then her ball zipped straight up a hippopotamus's tongue for a hole-in-one.

She stepped aside, secure in the fact that there was no way he was going to match her score on this round. "Let's see how you do."

"I plan to get a lot of use out of my ball on this hole," he said as he placed it on the green outdoor carpet. He carefully lined up his shot. "I like to ensure I get full value from my entertainment dollar." There was a twinkle in his eye as he hit the ball in what Zoe confidently knew was the wrong direction to get anything close to her results. The ball ricocheted off the course's edging and went in a side hole she hadn't known existed, putting him significantly below par for his own hole-in-one.

"Nice job, Ash."

His head jerked up at how she'd shortened his name. She had once called him that, and it had felt natural, but now, with him looking at her, she felt self-conscious, as if it was too much, too soon. Too significant.

"Is it okay if I call you that?" she asked.

"Be my guest."

Before Zoe could feel nervous, Ashton's cell phone rang. He pulled it out and frowned at caller ID before pocketing the device again.

"Who is it?" Zoe asked.

"Quentin."

"Answer it!"

Ashton moved nervously, finding his way off the course, muttering as he retrieved his phone again, "Is it too early to start drinking?"

His whole demeanor had changed, and it was like he was suddenly carrying the burden of the world upon his shoulders, that sorrow from last week returning.

"He probably just forgot how to put the car seat in again or something," Ashton said as he answered.

She knew it had to be almost impossible for him to walk away from Jaelyn, but at the same time she feared he was going to turn his back on Quentin and Jaelyn's needs—just like he had done to her last summer.

Zoe allowed a family to play through while she waited for Ashton, who had moved to the shade of the ice cream stand, phone lifted to his ear, head bent. She stepped a little closer to see if she could catch snippets of the conversation.

Ashton ended the call and came over.

"Everything okay?" she asked.

His jaw was tight as he took his golf club from her. "He wants me to babysit."

"Why?"

"I don't know." He was squeezing the golf club like he wanted to strike something with it, and Zoe hoped he didn't hate giraffes—the animal for the impossible sixth hole, where last year they'd each needed nine shots to complete their turns.

"He didn't say?"

"I didn't let him. My scheduled visitations are over, and it's just too darn hard seeing her, making her cry when I leave. It's for the best…" His shoulders were drooped, his face a mask of anguish.

"Did he say who might be looking for him at the cottages?"

Ashton didn't answer. He'd gone still, his brow pinched. "He thinks he can just call me up, tell me it's my problem to solve, just like Maliki." He straightened, staring at Zoe.

"I'm sorry he thinks he can use you," she said.

"I'm going to take a break from golf for a bit." Without waiting for her to reply he took a stool at the ice cream stand at the edge of the course.

Zoe followed him. Maybe this was why they never went back to the places they'd enjoyed. It was never as good the second time.

She settled onto the vacant stool beside him.

"I'm tired of people taking advantage of my kindness," he said, as soon as she sat down. "They aren't kidding when they say nice guys finish last, and that's all I ever seem to do. It's not Jaelyn's fault that Quentin's her real father and I'm not. The situation is impossible."

Zoe rested a hand on his shoulder and he seemed to snap out of it, saying, "I'm sorry."

"Do you want some ice cream?"

"What?"

She gestured to the teen waiting to take their order.

Ashton shook his head. "Do you?"

She shook her head as well, and the teen moved down the stand to serve a family.

Ashton stared at Zoe for a long moment, then let out an extended breath. He wrapped his arms around her, hugging her tight. "I am sorry. I'm spoiling our day."

She pulled back to look at him. "I happen to like that you're a nice guy. And please know that there are more people who appreciate that trait than there are who want to take advantage of it."

"It doesn't feel like it."

"That's only because you're in the middle of a big storm. Together we're going to find a way to get you out of it. Starting Monday. But right now, you're mine for the weekend. So let's forget about the rest of the world and enjoy ourselves."

* * *

ASHTON WAS angry at himself as well as Quentin. He was supposed to be enjoying a lovely weekend with Zoe, where they could patch fences, mend bridges or whatever the expression was. He was supposed to be winning her back. Instead he was fuming over the guy's lack of responsibility and worrying about Jaelyn. He'd bet anything Quentin had told his friend that he'd meet him at the Indigo Bay Cottages, where he'd drop off Jaelyn for some free babysitting courtesy of Ashton, and then he and his buddy could go out on a wild adventure, child-free.

Ashton was not going to be used, and he wasn't going to allow Jaelyn to be jerked back and forth like that.

Knowing he was distracted and edgy, he took Zoe's hand

across the table, and her features softened as she smiled at him.

This was what he needed to focus on. Zoe. Not everything that was whirling through his mind, or the way his stomach flipped over whenever he thought of Jaelyn.

Zoe had called him Ash again. That was what he needed to remember. That and the fact that she wanted to be here with him, and nobody else. No problems, just the two of them.

"As your official bodyguard, shall I walk you back to your room?" he asked as he stood, giving a gallant bow. They'd had a relatively early supper thanks to his quitting mini golf early, and now had numerous empty evening hours to fill, which had never been an issue in the past. But with how edgy he was, he knew in a way he'd just blown the weekend for Zoe.

She tucked her arm through his, feeling so natural and right that he wanted to stop and kiss her until they both forgot the past, forgot everything but each other and she begged him to take her home. Instead, he kept it all inside as they moved through the clubhouse toward the outer doors.

"It will be Sunday night when we get back to Indigo Bay," he said, once they were outside.

Zoe stopped a step above him, looking as though she expected him to continue with his line of thought.

"I was thinking maybe we could order in pizza and watch a movie. Like old times." He brushed a strand of hair from her face, wanting to kiss her perfect cherry lips.

Her eyes lit up for a second before she dampened her excitement, pulling away ever so slightly.

"What's wrong?"

"Maybe we need new habits," she said.

He was worried this was going to turn into a breakup—before it had even become a true relationship. Either that or she was trying to outwit the future and any possible repeated mistakes by giving up on old routines. Routines that had brought them closer together the first time around.

"Are you okay?"

She shook her head, her curls tumbling over her shoulders, her long lashes brushing her pale cheeks as though she was summoning an inner resolve to be strong.

"I want you back in my life," she admitted. "But I'm scared."

"I want you back in mine, too."

Her glossy lips parted as she whispered, "If we're honestly pursuing this again, then I need to know that you're not going to shut me out. I know I said I don't want to bring your problems into our weekend, but I can tell you're thinking about Jaelyn and Quentin and that you're worried about them. So I suppose I'm saying let's be in this together. If you need to talk about it, let's talk about it."

Yup. He was blowing the weekend despite his attempts not to.

"And know that I'm here. Even when I'm not poking and prodding. And if you want to talk even though I said let's not —you can."

"I know."

She waited.

"I'm here for you," she added.

Ashton took her in his arms. "I'm here for you, too." He met her gaze as he said, "*Always*."

"I think you need to say yes to babysitting Jaelyn."

Ashton dropped his arms and involuntarily stepped back. "What?"

"What if you were the best thing in her life?"

"I'm not welcome in her life any longer, and I make it difficult for her when I leave. It's traumatic. For both of us.

She's bonded with Quentin now, and she can't count on me to be there for her. Not with Quentin wanting me out."

"But doesn't he want you back in?"

"For how long, though? Does he just want a sitter so he can go party, or whatever it is he does? I can't do that. I can't bear to just *leave* her. It's not fair to her." Or him. It could break him just like losing Zoe had nearly broken him.

"What if something's going on with him? What if Jaelyn needs you? What if she needs a stable adult in her life?"

Ashton felt the cold hand of dread give him a squeeze. He hated that rational, smart Zoe might be fearing the worst, too.

"The courts found him fit," he said, his voice uneven. The temptation to swoop back into Jaelyn's life was unbearably strong.

"We should call someone," Zoe prodded. "Have them check in on her."

Despite the pain, Ashton met Zoe's eyes and nodded. He could alleviate his worries without being used or making things hard on Jaelyn. "I have a friend in social services. Maybe he can check on them."

* * *

Zoe paced her room at the bed-and-breakfast after a few rounds of backgammon in the games area. Ashton had asked his social worker buddy to check in on Jaelyn, and the friend had logged into the system while on the phone with him, reporting that someone had just been by for a home checkup not that long ago. And that unless Ashton had something more worrisome than the father asking him to babysit, it was time to leave well enough alone. By the sound of it, it wasn't the first time Ashton had called in a favor on Jaelyn's behalf.

He'd then called Quentin back, leaving a message on the man's voice mail. He'd texted, too. No reply.

Maliki didn't have family other than an aunt in Seattle, and he'd quickly reached a dead end in regards to people who might be able to give him answers.

By the end of the evening, Zoe had ended up feeling as antsy as Ashton who was regretting not prying more from Quentin when he'd had him on the line. She had given Ashton a goodnight kiss that she wished had been as carefree as it had been last summer, and then turned in early.

Why was that man looking for Quentin? And why was Quentin *really* looking for Ashton? Was it simply for babysitting? If so, why not ask friends or family?

Something had to be up.

And while Ashton wasn't getting anywhere with his personal connections, maybe Zoe could with hers. Mind made up, she picked up her cell phone, telling herself that she was interfering only because she wanted a true second chance with Ashton, and that the only way to do that was to get to the bottom of this.

She dialed Dallas Harper first. "Dallas, it's Zoe. I need a favor."

"Anything for my favorite employee. Did Margie tell you that your newsletter has already increased rebookings?"

"That's great." She began pacing again, her free hand flexing. "Remember that guy who came up to my desk while you were trying to convince me to start the newsletter?"

"Not really."

"He was looking for someone named Quentin Valant. He's come in a few times, but there's never anyone registered under that name."

"Not ringing any bells. Wait. Isn't that the guy who left a message for Ashton?"

"Quentin was, but this other guy is a mystery."

"Is Ashton in trouble?" She could hear the note of alarm in Dallas's voice.

"I don't think so, but I need to find out if the little girl he was helping is."

"Why don't you ask Ashton about these guys?" Dallas asked carefully.

"He's trying to get answers, but I have a feeling whoever that dude is, he's someone who could cause trouble."

"So, just to be clear," Dallas said, "you're not asking me to break any guest confidentiality or privacy laws. You're simply inquiring about a resort security issue."

"Yes. Exactly." He was the best boss ever. "I'm hoping that someone can find security footage and send me a good picture of the guy."

"Send it to *you*?"

Was that pushing it too far?

"I'll forward it to a man who can figure out who this guy is."

She knew Ginger's husband was working as a private security agent these days. He could either help her or would know someone who could.

After hanging up with Dallas, Zoe called Ginger. "I hate to ask for favors," she said after their niceties. "But I need one."

"Oh, goody," Ginger said. Zoe could practically see her in her mind's eye, rubbing her hands, obviously thinking her matchmaking skills were in need. "I recommend a candlelight dinner on the beach."

"Not that kind of favor. I need one from Logan."

"Is everything all right?"

"There's this guy who's been asking for someone I know, and I was hoping Logan could put a name to the face. Is he able to do something like that?"

"Sure. Do you have a picture?"

"Not yet. Dallas is working on it."

"I'll forward you his email. He loves working on stuff like this. Thanks for thinking of him." She added, "Are you sure everything is all right?"

"I don't know," Zoe answered truthfully.

"Well, best to find out then," Ginger replied. "Logan's good. And if he can't track this guy, his partner, Zach Forrester, can."

Zoe ended the call, hoping Ashton wouldn't be too upset with her when he found out she'd started digging into his life.

But she already knew that it was always best to know the truth, even if it sometimes hurt.

CHAPTER 7

Ashton hadn't heard anything from Quentin since the weekend, and Zoe said nobody had come looking for him again. Ashton had a feeling he'd been right. Quentin had simply been planning a guys' getaway, but hadn't counted on him saying no to taking care of Jaelyn.

Which meant Ashton could now focus solely on Zoe and his future, and stop worrying about Jaelyn—or at least not as much.

He set down his coffee in Zoe's gazebo and looked at the flyer for the Indigo Bay hardware store that she was pointing to. "I found a housewarming gift for you," she said, her smile so pretty and open it nearly took his breath away. "Do you have one of these?"

It was a power drill.

"I don't."

Ashton had helped Zoe move back into her fixed-up house yesterday, and she was still unpacking, her cats delighted to be home, and among so many boxes to hide in. Ashton had come over to help her move a large dresser that morning because Binx kept using it to launch himself at the window screen in her bedroom. Ashton had ended up staying for coffee.

"I decided not to buy the place," he said, surprised at how offhand he sounded.

"Why not?"

"It didn't feel as though the timing was right."

Zoe watched him for a moment, no doubt trying to decipher the meaning behind his unannounced change of plans, and possibly fearing he was preparing to leave her again.

He wasn't. Quite the opposite. All week he'd come by to share her afternoon break with her, and they often sought each other out more evenings than not. All that had done was solidify the fact that he knew he was meant to be with Zoe. And that meant he wanted to find a way to ensure he had as much time freed up to spend with her in the future as possible.

"What happened?" she asked. "What changed?"

"I calculated how long the renovations would take." As a teacher he had a lot of time in the summer, but once he was back at school his evenings and weekends were generally booked up with grading and lesson planning. "There are other things I'd rather do over the next few years instead of spending every free moment covered in construction dust."

He could see Zoe visibly relax. She *had* been worried he was going to leave her. Ashton set down his cup and reached across the slated wood table to caress the top of her hand. "I'm in town to stay, even if I don't buy that time-suck of a house."

"How do you plan to spend all that newfound dust-free time?" She was flirting with him and he couldn't fight the smile that came to his lips.

"With a beautiful woman."

She smiled back. Her expression suddenly changing as though remembering something and checked her phone for the time before standing up. "Speaking of beautiful women, I need to meet with a bride-to-be in fifteen minutes." She brushed the wrinkles from her linen shorts. "I have to scoot." She dusted his lips with a kiss, then hurried out of the gazebo.

"Lock up when you leave?" she called over her shoulder.

"I'll clean up, too," he said wryly, holding up their empty coffee cups.

* * *

Zoe sat in her car for a moment before she started the engine, then pulled away from the curb, heading to work. Ashton had relaxed since their weekend away, and so had she, as nothing had popped up on the Quentin radar. She ought to tell Logan that he and his pal Zach could cease their quest to match the grainy footage from the resort's security camera to a real man: the one with the scar.

She loved the new, gentle routine that she and Ashton were settling into. This time would be different, because they were different. And she was finding it difficult not to indulge in fantasies of their lives intertwined, his strong arms wrapped around her. His hot lips blazing trails down her neck. Waking up next to him, already smiling because they were together again at last.

She needed to slow down. Take her time.

But she didn't want to. She wanted to zoom ahead.

Zoe sighed as she parked her car at work, nudging the Staff Only sign and bending its metal pole in the process. She reversed her vehicle. She was definitely distracted by thoughts of Ashton.

"Did you just do that?" Dallas asked as he walked past,

lunch bag in hand. He had his eyebrows raised as he took in the bent parking sign.

Zoe winced, coming around her car to check the damage. "Maybe."

"You need to get your head back on straight," he said kindly, slinging his arm across her shoulders and giving her a small shake before they parted ways, him taking one tree-lined brick trail toward his office while she headed along the wider path toward the main building.

"Tell me about it," she muttered to herself.

Once at her desk, she booted up her computer and checked the last-minute details she planned to go over with the bride and groom-to-be. She looked up as a shadow crossed her desk, expecting it to be the wedding couple.

It was the man with the scar who kept asking for Quentin. Zoe's stomach dropped.

It wasn't over. Whatever "it" was.

"Can I help you?" she asked, her hands shaking with nerves.

"I'm looking for Quentin Valant." He gave her a charming smile. "Again."

"Of course. Let me see if he's checked in." Zoe tried to maintain a neutral expression instead of a panicked one as she pulled up the reservation list. Why did he think Quentin was going to show up here? And was that reason related to Ashton?

"Planning to do some fishing?" she asked, before scanning the list for a name she knew wouldn't be there.

"Maybe." He casually leaned against her desk, taking in the lobby while he waited.

"I'm sorry, there's still no reservation by that last name."

The man inhaled while straightening, looking thoughtful.

Shoot. She should have said he was here, then asked for

this guy's name so she could pass on whatever message he had. Some spy she made—not that she wanted to be one.

"Why not try Dianne Thomas," the man said smoothly.

She checked the computer. "Sorry, nothing."

"Ashton Wallace?"

Zoe froze. He'd asked for Ashton. Her Ashton. Her body, like it was on autopilot, stiffly turned back to the computer.

"Let me just see," she said cheerfully. She made a show of checking the reservation list, all the while her heart thundering so hard she was afraid he would hear it.

"Oh!" She hoped her fake surprise was believable. "He has a booking. Would you like to leave a message?" She picked up a pencil, found it was broken, and picked up another. "Who shall I say is wanting to get in touch?"

"Which room?" The man had honed in on her, and she felt like she was about to be eviscerated. She'd done the wrong thing. She'd told him Ashton was here, and that had made him a target.

"We can't give out that information."

The man stepped away from the desk, his eyes roaming the lobby as if he was searching for a place to start overturning the resort.

"He's checking out this morning," Zoe said quickly. "Why not leave a message with me, and I'll make sure it gets to him."

"He's checking out?" He was focusing on her again, and it felt as though the building's air conditioning had broken.

"Yes."

The man made a move toward her desk, as if planning to flip her monitor to face him. She exited the reservations program just in case, her body vibrating with awareness of how this could all go wrong. And quickly.

The man trained his eyes on hers and she found herself leaning away.

"Would you like to leave a message?" she asked again. *Pretend everything is normal.*

Everything *could* be normal.

"Tell Ashton I'm looking for Quentin."

"Sure. And who are you?" Zoe asked, pencil poised over the paper. Her hand was shaking so badly she feared she wouldn't be able to write legibly.

The man was staring at her. He'd noted the shaking.

"It's palsy," she lied. "It gets worse with age. I'll be a trembling wreck by the time I'm sixty."

He met her eyes again. "He'll know who I am."

"Ashton will?"

"Tell him Quentin needs to cover his expenses."

"Right. Cover his expenses." She scrawled on the paper, shivers shooting up her spine. "Will he know for what?"

The man was already stalking off, hands deep in his pockets. He nodded politely at Margie as he passed the front desk, and Zoe quickly went back into the reservations system and changed the name on Ashton's booking to the first thing that came to mind: Bugs Bunny. She followed that up with a quick email to staff alerting them to be on the lookout for the man with the scar, and to be extra vigilant about not releasing guest information to anyone who approached them.

An email immediately dinged back from Dallas, but Zoe's finger was already poised over the Log Out button. As she tapped it her monitor went to the lock screen, and she hurried to the parking lot to see if she could snag a plate number—something, anything to help Logan track this man faster.

All she saw was a black Ford Escape leaving the lot.

She ran back to her desk, where she called security to save the lobby camera's footage of the man with the scar, then contacted Logan to tell him to hurry up with his digging.

Next she called Ashton. As he picked up she saw the bride-to-be enter the lobby, looking around for her. Zoe gave a little wave to catch her attention, then held up a finger while turning away slightly to speak with Ashton.

"Ashton?" She held the phone tight to her ear as though afraid someone would eavesdrop. "That guy was here asking for Quentin. And you."

"Did he leave a name?"

"No." She described the man and the message he'd left.

She could hear Ashton inhale slowly.

"What's going on?" she asked him. "Who is this guy?"

"I'm not sure." There was a wariness in his voice and she knew immediately that he was thinking hard, plus holding things back.

"Why does he keep coming here? Why is he looking for you?" She flashed a smile over her shoulder to the waiting bride and groom, and mouthed *"sorry"* before turning away again.

"I don't know."

"He said you would."

"I think it might be this guy who came by the apartment once. I didn't like the feel of him."

"I don't, either. Where are you?"

"Washing your dishes. And being mauled by Mishka who apparently loves dish bubbles. Are you cats allowed on the counters?"

"No. And just...stay there. I told him you were checking out this morning. He's looking for you and I'm pretty sure he's driving a black Ford Escape."

"Okay."

"Ashton?"

"Yeah?"

"I think it's time to call the police."

"And tell them what? That this guy keeps looking for this other guy who, from the sounds of things, owes him money? That's not against the law." Despite his logic and even voice, she could hear the uncertainty hiding underneath.

"They're involving you."

"Quentin must have told him I'm here, and that he planned to come here, too. Maybe he'd planned for me to babysit so he could work and pay off the debt or something. I'll try calling Quentin again and get to the bottom of this. And if that guy comes by again, give him my number. I'll get this sorted out, Zoe."

She nodded, relieved by his get-it-solved attitude. He wasn't hiding anything, and he wasn't avoiding anything, either.

"What if Quentin doesn't answer your call?" she asked.

"Then I'll drive to the city and track him down."

"Be careful. Let me know where you are."

"I will."

The building's air conditioning suddenly seemed to be doing too fine a job, and Zoe shivered.

* * *

"YOU HAD LOGAN DO WHAT?" Ashton blinked hard, trying to understand what Zoe was saying. It sounded a lot like she'd had someone spy on him—well, on the man looking for him. He wasn't sure whether to be pleased, relieved or indignant that she'd kept that from him.

He'd spent the afternoon trying to chase down Quentin, without success. Endless phone calls and driving around the city. Nobody had seen Quentin or Jaelyn in days, and an ever-increasing feeling of unease had settled over Ashton. He was *this* close to filing a missing persons report.

He'd come by the rented cottage to grab a few things before heading over to Zoe's to spend the night on her couch, but she'd met him here, unable to await his arrival.

"I had him try and find out who that guy is," she explained, as she laid out a pile of receipts with handwritten notes on the back as if she'd had nothing else to scrawl upon. "His name is Morty Gallagher and he's a wanted felon."

Ashton blinked once. Twice.

"Morty's been coming by the resort?" After hearing Zoe's description of him earlier that day, he'd been really hoping that there was more than one man with a facial scar in Quentin's life and that it had not, in fact, been Morty.

Ashton had met him once, when the man had stopped by the apartment shortly after Maliki had passed on, asking for the whereabouts of Quentin. Despite his charming smile, he'd made Jaelyn cry just by looking at her. He'd asked where Maliki was, too, and when he'd heard that she'd died, he'd asked if she'd left anything for him. The way he'd said it had made Ashton nervous. Nervous enough that he'd started looking for somewhere new to live. But then Quentin had come to claim Jaelyn and was deemed fit, and Ashton hadn't thought about it much further.

"This guy—Morty Gallagher—has a major record," Zoe said. "So does Quentin. And they think you know something."

"I don't."

"Why is Morty looking for Quentin? Why does he think he's with you?"

Why indeed? Ashton mulled over her questions, the hairs on the back of his neck standing on end.

"No wonder I couldn't find Quentin and Jaelyn," he mused. "They're probably hiding."

"We need to call the police," Zoe stated.

Ashton nodded. He looked at the notes she'd laid out on

his kitchen counter. He had a feeling his life was about to take an unwanted detour again. One away from Zoe.

He fished out his cell phone. "I'll try Quentin one more time, okay?"

His call went to voice mail. He tried again, desperate to hear the man's voice.

"Come on, pick up the phone," he muttered. Voice mail again.

Zoe's gaze was trained on her notes. "We should go back to my place. Call the police from there."

"Hey," he said, pulling her into his arms, trying to quell her fears. "It'll all work out. I'll keep you safe, I promise." He'd do whatever he needed to do to protect her. Her and Jaelyn.

Zoe nodded, then pushed away. She swept the receipts into a bundle and jammed them into her pockets. "Let's go before this wind brings a deluge."

He picked up the bag he'd packed, but as he stepped onto the porch ahead of Zoe, a dark SUV came along the trail that served as the cottage's long driveway. The hairs on Ashton's neck lifted again and he retreated, knocking Zoe back over the threshold.

He continued propelling her deeper into the cottage until she was at the back door. He opened it for her, then pushed her outside.

"You need to go."

* * *

THE BREEZE off the ocean had increased and it ruffled Zoe's hair as she stood, stunned, on the back porch of the purple cottage. She'd seen the black Escape. She knew who was inside.

She clung to Ashton's shirt. "I want to stay. You shouldn't be alone."

"I don't think that's a good idea." He was trying to close the door on her, gently removing her hand from his cotton garment. "You need to go home. Away from here."

"But—"

"You lied to him today," he said firmly, his expression closed and so like it had been when he'd come back from Charleston last August to break up with her. "You told him I'd left, and now he's here. Stay out of this."

"I was trying to protect you."

"And now I'm trying to protect *you*."

"Protection means sharing. Working together, supporting each other, and you're shutting me out. We're supposed to share everything if we're a couple."

"You don't know what these men are like."

"Because you won't tell me! I had to hire Logan to find out!"

"Why would I drag you into a mess, Zoe? You don't do that to someone you..."

Ashton drew up short, letting out an anguished, shaky breath, his gaze averted.

Zoe froze, his unfinished statement hanging like a knife over her heart. You shared your burdens when you loved someone. And he wasn't sharing. So what was he saying? He didn't love her? She'd felt his love. So why couldn't he let her in? Was their love ever going to be strong enough that he'd trust her to help with the hard stuff life threw their way?

"I'm trying to prevent you from being hurt," he said carefully.

"Well, you're a little too late for that." Zoe turned on her heel and scuttled down the steps with tears in her eyes. "Good luck on your own."

"Zoe," he called, reluctance in his tone.

"No. You don't want me here, then fine. I won't help. You

just keep on keeping your secrets. I thought we'd changed and we haven't."

She swiped a hand across her eyes as she stormed off, sand stinging her bare ankles as the wind whipped the loose grains against her. She vowed that her tears would be the last ones she ever shed for Ashton Wallace.

* * *

ASHTON DIDN'T HAVE time to think about what had just happened between him and Zoe, or how hurt she'd looked as he'd tried to shield her from whatever was about to go down on his front step. He knew Zoe didn't understand, but he'd do whatever he had to in order to keep her off Morty's radar, because he'd learned that simply answering the door one fine afternoon had put him on the watch list for a man who had a criminal record longer than his own years of education.

Ashton headed to the front door, half expecting to see Zoe come tearing around the side of the building to give Morty what-for.

"You're a hard man to find," his visitor said casually, his boot heels crunching as he made his way up the crushed-shell driveway. The wind was tugging at his clothing, sand hissing as it moved.

"I didn't realize you were looking."

Morty huffed in disbelief, his gaze seeming to catch something to the side of the cottage, where wild grasses were bending in the wind. Ashton hoped Zoe had cleared the area.

She felt that protection meant sharing, but any interaction with a man like Morty wasn't something you wished upon someone you loved. The man had already approached Zoe several times while at her desk, and it wouldn't be long before he realized she'd lied in order to shield Ashton. And that was enough for a guy like Morty to use her as leverage to force Ashton to get Quentin for him.

She needed to stay out of the picture until this was settled.

A flicker of warning flashed in Ashton's mind—she might continue to remain out of the picture after that goodbye.

"What can I do for you?" he asked, as Morty stepped closer.

"Quentin has something of mine."

"Oh?"

"Where is he?"

"I don't know."

Morty was up the steps in a flash and pressing a knife against Ashton's throat. Ashton hadn't even tried to move, knowing that running would only make him appear guilty.

Ashton prayed Zoe wasn't watching, and that if she was, she wouldn't get any bright ideas about being helpful.

"Why is he in Indigo Bay?" Morty asked.

"I don't know that he is," Ashton said carefully. The blade pressed into his flesh whenever his jaw moved. "He hasn't approached me. We're not friends."

"I've pulled his records. He's called you."

Ashton went to nod, then thought better of moving. "Yes."

"What did he say?"

"He's looking for a babysitter."

"Is that code for something?"

"I don't think so." He hated referencing Jaelyn in case Morty got a brilliant idea about how he could leverage her to force Quentin to do his bidding, whatever that might be.

"Where is he staying?" The blade pressed closer.

"I don't know. I'm sorry. Really. I went looking today, but I've mostly been trying to avoid him and the trouble that follows." Ashton met Morty's eye, relieved when the man's showed a glitter of amusement.

"I see that's worked out well for you." He lowered the knife, taking half a step back. His feet were braced and he was clearly ready to make a move as soon as Ashton did.

Ashton didn't plan on moving until the man and his vehicle were long gone.

"You have a woman covering for you," Morty stated.

Ashton knew better than to reply, and he hoped his face didn't show the fear he felt for Zoe. But Morty was smart, and Ashton could see it in his gaze and the way it flicked over him, catching nuances in his body language.

"Send Quentin to me," Morty said in a low voice, thick with meaning, "and she won't get hurt."

"He's not answering my calls," Ashton said. "And the woman has nothing to do with this."

"No," Morty said, stepping back into Ashton's face with a wave of stale breath. "She has everything to do with this if I don't get what I want."

"What is it you want?" Ashton spoke directly. He needed this resolved so he could move on with his life. His life with Zoe.

Safely.

Everything over and done with.

"Quentin knows," Morty said grimly. His footsteps were heavy on the cottage's weathered steps as he moved to his SUV, which sent shells flying as he spun out of the driveway and into the darkening night.

CHAPTER 8

Ashton had spent hours pacing his rented cottage. He'd called the police, but it turned out Zoe already had on his behalf—he'd left her a voice mail warning her about Morty when she didn't pick up. The police had said to call if Morty or Quentin tried to contact him again, and that they'd put out an all points bulletin for Quentin and Jaelyn. He'd requested they watch Zoe's house, too, but they were understaffed for a 24/7 watch, though they'd promised to check in on her whenever they could.

Beyond that, Ashton didn't know what to do. He'd left yet another message on Quentin's phone, but hadn't heard back. There was no point hiding from Morty now that the man had found him. And there was definitely no reason to make Zoe an even bigger target by going to her house to talk.

Ashton lay on his bed, fully clothed, and tugged the blanket up to his shoulders, listening to rain approach on the wind, then move on. Around one in the morning there was a knock at his door. He froze for a moment, contemplating his options; before he got out of bed and hurried through the cottage to look out the window.

It was Quentin standing on his front porch, looking as antsy as a raccoon being circled by a pack of wolves.

"Where have you been?" Ashton demanded as he opened the door. The salty, earthy smell of ocean and rain entered on a breeze. "I've been trying to call you."

"I have to lie low for a while," the man said, his eyes shifting as quickly as his weight moved from foot to foot.

"Lay low?" Ashton was unable to prevent the contempt from edging into his voice. Quentin was supposed to be a good dad for Jaelyn. Good dads who'd cleaned up their lives didn't have to lie low. They also didn't come to someone's door at one in the morning unless they were seeking children's Tylenol.

Quentin looked up, his Adam's apple bobbing, his eyes big. He looked scared. "Yeah. For a while."

"You're a dad."

"I know."

"You took Jaelyn from me. You said you wanted a clean life. That you were ready."

"I know."

"But you brought Morty to my door, and I hate to think what kind of life you're creating for Jaelyn. Morty's threatened me and my girlfriend because of you. And this would be the same girlfriend I had to leave in order to fix the big mess you left Maliki in." Ashton stepped onto the lit porch, sending moths fluttering around the light above him. Quentin backed away to the edge of the steps. "And now you're here messing things up once again. I don't know what's happening with you and Morty, only that it's encroaching into my life. Again."

"Jaelyn needs you," Quentin said, his head bowed.

Ashton hesitated, the anger that was building inside him shifting to roiling frustration. He wanted to tell Quentin to take a hike and to stop messing with his life. But Jaelyn... She was an innocent in all this and deserved a perfect, secure life.

He wanted to flatten Quentin, then haul him back up onto his feet and force him to be the man Jaelyn deserved.

Quentin reached inside his leather jacket, then handed Ashton a large, thick envelope.

"What's this?"

"Your name is still on her birth certificate."

Ashton tried to pass the papers back. "You said you were going to file the change after we saw the notary."

"I didn't."

"What game are you playing?"

"I tried." Quentin bounced from foot to foot. "I tried playing it straight, and being a dad. And I can't. I just can't. My daughter deserves better. She deserves her real father."

"Then be that man."

"She deserves you. You stepped up when I didn't." Quentin glanced over his shoulder. "Can I come in?"

Ashton widened his stance. "Why?"

"Are you going to take her, or do I need to abandon her?" Quentin's movements had become even more agitated.

"You're serious." Ashton's heart was starting to hammer.

"I've got to lay low, man. Like, right now. Jae deserves a proper life, not what I have to offer."

"If you're saying what I think you are...how am I supposed to keep her safe? You made me a target."

Quentin was shaking his head furiously. "No. No. I'll pay my debts. I just have to...quietly earn back the cash I owe. He won't have a reason to come after her. But I can't do this and be a good dad."

Ashton cursed under his breath. Quentin might actually be putting Jaelyn's needs ahead of everything. But after all the hurt Ashton had gone through over the past few months, only to have it all reversed on him...he wasn't certain he could bear it if Quentin reclaimed Jaelyn again. And he surely would. Again and again, because Ashton was a nice guy who fixed things, and a man who couldn't say no where Jaelyn's safety and well-being was concerned. And Quentin knew it.

"I'm not interested in taking her just to have you come along and whisk her away again," Ashton explained steadily. "That's no way for a kid to grow up."

"I signed over my rights." Quentin was soberly staring at the envelope in Ashton's hands.

Ashton opened the end of the envelope and pulled out the contents. There were a lot of official looking papers, several of them with the logo of a Charleston lawyer. His mouth felt dry. This was what he wanted, but it still felt wrong somehow.

"You can come back at any time and have all of this reversed," he said hoarsely. "I'm not interested in being jerked around."

He went to shove the papers at Quentin, but the man moved down the steps, opening the back door of his car. He ducked inside as he said, "I won't be coming back. Not this time."

"How can I be sure?" Ashton found himself moving closer to the vehicle.

Quentin straightened, his expression one of determination, a sleepy Jaelyn in his arms. She saw Ashton and her face broke into a big, toothy grin as she squealed, "Da!" She lunged forward, arms outstretched.

With resignation, Quentin said, "You'll always be her real dad."

And as Ashton reached for the little girl, he knew the man was right.

* * *

ZOE KEPT PACING the area behind her guest services desk. She hadn't been able to sleep, and the idea of the police cruising by her home all night to check on her was unsettling. So at the crack of dawn she'd given up and come in to work.

But she couldn't sit still, couldn't wrap her mind around the fact that Ashton had let her walk away last night. No, *pushed* her away. Again.

He'd said he was trying to protect her, but that's not how relationships worked. Her parents didn't shut each other out and they were the gold standard when it came to relationships. Ashton just wasn't willing to let Zoe in when it really mattered.

"You're here extra early," said a familiar voice. "Which is great because I have some good news to share."

Zoe glanced over to find Dallas on the other side of her desk, grinning at her. She checked the clock as his smile faded. It was only seven-fifteen. It was going to be a long day.

"You okay?" he asked.

She brightened falsely, smoothing her khakis. "Yes, of course. What's the good news?"

Dallas paused before saying, "You know that big wedding you were hoping to land here at the resort? Well…" He held out his arms. "Guess what? I just signed a contract with the happy couple. They'll be phoning you later today to work on details."

Zoe wanted to be excited. The last time she'd helped coordinate something large had been at Christmas, when Luke Cohen and Emma Carrington had filled the town with close to five hundred guests, booking just about every room and cottage in the resort, as well as several other places in town. She'd worked with Luke's assistant, Alexa McTavish, to ensure everything went smoothly with the party over at the Portia House mansion, and the experience had been a fun challenge. But today she simply didn't have the energy to even contemplate handling such a large event.

"It sounds like you may become the resort's official wedding coordinator if these contracts keep continuing."

"Yeah, of course. Great," she said absently, as she shifted from foot to foot. How could she continue to coordinate something like this when she didn't even know what it was like to find someone committed enough to actually make it down the aisle with her?

She used to strive to give her brides and grooms the perfect launch into marital harmony and wedded bliss, but now it felt as if every happy couple was rubbing salt in her wounds and pointing big, flashing arrows at the one thing she'd never have.

Dallas began humming the "Wedding March" and Zoe tumbled into her office chair, her eyes welling with tears.

"Overcome with gratitude and excitement?"

"Yeah, it's great." Her voice sounded high-pitched and pained.

"What's wrong?" Dallas asked. He leaned against her desk, his brow furrowing with concern.

"Nothing," Zoe said, wiping her cheeks as tears overflowed.

"That's not nothing."

"I'm fine, really."

"Is this about—"

"It's fine," Zoe said, a bit sharply.

Dallas gave her a long look, hands raised, before walking away, saying over his shoulder, "You know where I am if you need anything."

Why was she falling apart? She'd *known* this was going to

happen with Ashton. Yet she couldn't help wondering if maybe she'd just pressed harder this time things would have worked out. But she was certain she'd done everything right. Not too fast, not too slow. She'd asked him to open up, but he'd pushed her out. He didn't trust her to truly have his back, and he likely never would.

As good as they were together, it just wasn't meant to be. Not long-term.

She had chosen to give him a second shot, knowing the risks. And it hadn't worked out.

Now it was time to get over him and move on.

* * *

ASHTON SURVEYED the cottage without truly seeing it as he walked the sleeping child in his arms back and forth. Jaelyn was his. That fact refused to sink in. She hadn't left with Quentin, but was right back where she'd always belonged —with him.

It was morning now, the world awakening. He'd called the police station again, and informed them there was also a child in need of protection now. They'd placed a patrol car out front for the night while they looked into things, debating the level of protection he might need long-term.

Ashton kept moving around the living room so Jaelyn would stay sleeping. She hadn't wanted to let him out of her sight. Whenever he put her down she broke his heart by crawling over and clinging to his leg, repeating, "Da."

He'd kept telling her he was staying. He was here. He wasn't going anywhere. But she didn't believe him. Their separation had obviously felt as long and painful to her as it had to him.

She'd grown, but she was still the same girl. Quentin had

handed her over with a stroller and car seat that Ashton had purchased months ago, as well as a bag of unfamiliar clothes. Four diapers. No carefully selected high chair. No playpen, no crib.

Ashton needed to go shopping. He needed a place he could child-proof. He needed a home.

He also needed a full-time contract with a school division, and Morty off his tail.

Would Quentin truly be able to resolve things now that he was childless?

Either way, Ashton had a daughter he needed to provide for as well as keep safe. How long until Morty came to his door again? What if he tried to take Jaelyn?

Ashton needed Zoe in his life, he needed Jaelyn, and he needed to protect them both, but he didn't know how. He picked up the phone and called the officer sitting outside the cottage.

* * *

ZOE SAT in the sand and stared out over the ocean. The waves kept rolling in, unrelenting, just like her doubts about breaking up with Ashton last night.

After talking to Dallas, she'd decided to request a mental health day, and by seven forty was sitting on the beach, trying to sort out her head.

Down near the tiki hut bar she could see a woman who reminded her of her mom, her gray curls lifting off her shoulders with each gust of ocean breeze. She could use someone like her to talk to, but her mother wasn't due back for another day or so from a cruise she'd taken with friends.

Last night Zoe had felt justified in demanding that Ashton let her be at his side as he faced Morty, then indignant when he'd tried to protect her. But now...not so much.

Yes, she feared he was keeping things from her, shutting her out again, but she also feared she had been unreasonable and had allowed the pain of the past to taint an entirely new situation.

Zoe continued to watch as the woman drew closer, then stood up and waved. It was her mom.

"Zoe! I was looking for you," her mom said as she approached. Zoe gave her a huge hug, happy to see her. "Your yard looks amazing. Did Ashton do that for you?"

Zoe nodded. It already felt like so long ago.

"I go away for two weeks and everything changes. Caroline said you two have been hanging out."

"Yeah. We were. When did you get back?"

"Last night." Her mom fell into step beside her, and they began walking the beach together. "Apparently I told everyone the wrong return date. I nearly gave your father a heart attack when I climbed into bed next to him." She giggled.

Her mom's steps suddenly faltered. "Wait. *Were* hanging out?"

Zoe sighed. "I think we broke up last night."

"Why?"

"I don't know. I really thought we had what you and Dad have."

"And what's that?"

"Something perfect."

Her mom laughed. "Perfect? Hardly, sweetie."

"It looks pretty perfect to me."

"You don't see us fight."

"You don't fight that often."

"True." She smiled, her love for her husband evident in her twinkling eyes. "But it's also not perfect."

"You two talk and share everything, though. You trust each other with the hard stuff."

"You and Ashton have only been together a short time."

"So?"

"So," her mother said carefully, "you aren't going to share everything immediately. It takes time to build that trust. But I saw last summer how much the two of you loved each other, and I know you will build that solid foundation you crave as you share your lives."

"But he's not sharing. I shouldn't have to hire an investigator to find out that the person looking for him is wanted by the police."

"You hired an investigator?"

"You share your life with the people you love. You don't keep secrets."

"Why was the man looking for him?"

"It's a really long story. He shuffled me out of his house as soon as he saw the man coming. I couldn't even…" She shook her head, her frustration and anger taking over again.

"Do you think maybe he was trying to protect you?"

"I thought we'd changed, Mom. I thought he was going to let me in this time."

"Don't you think you're expecting too much in too short of a time frame? Two weeks, honey. After almost a year apart."

"But if he's really The One, it should be easy. Like it is for you and Dad."

"It's not easy, and your dad doesn't know everything about me, and I don't know everything about him. But it's *okay*. I trust him and he trusts me."

Zoe came up short. "Like what? What doesn't he know?"

"Well…" Her mother was hedging, making Zoe all the more curious. "Sometimes there's no need to overshare," she said simply.

"What is it?" How could her parents, who seemed to know everything about each other, have secrets?

"He doesn't know I broke up with my first boyfriend because he treated me poorly."

"Why didn't you let him know?"

"I was protecting him."

"From what?"

"From going and beating up the guy and getting charged with assault." She let out a sigh, then laughed. "And anyway, I just wanted to move past it. Now it's old news."

"But wasn't that lying?"

"If he'd asked, or if it had come up by way of conversation, I would have told him. But there was no point telling him about something that would only cause an upset. He'd have thought less of me, too, I feared."

"Why?"

"For letting him speak so poorly to me."

"It doesn't work that way, Mom."

"I know. But it's how I *feel*. And anyway, I think you're dad basically figured it out."

"But don't you worry that he thinks you don't trust him?"

"No." Her mother bent down to pick up a white shell. "We're also a lot stronger now than we were back then. We've had time to build a foundation of trust and honesty. We look out for each other. But that doesn't mean it's all black-and-white." She swatted at the air as though batting the topic away. "Anyway, he'd probably laugh and call me a silly goose for worrying about it after all this time. It's so minor."

Was that all she and Ashton needed? Time? Time to build more trust in each other?

She thought of Ashton, and how he'd said he was trying to protect her. Maybe she'd deliberately blinded herself to his intentions, taking her past wounds and making the moment

about them and her fears instead of what was really happening
—the way he was sheltering her from possible danger.

That was something you did for someone you loved.

Zoe had been so certain she was right, but maybe Ashton
was, too.

"Do you think I pulled the trigger too quickly?" she asked
her mom, wincing as she waited for the answer.

"Of course I do. You're single and regretting it, are
you not?"

And that she was. It was just a matter of what to do
about it.

* * *

Officer Ben Andrews was standing in the cottage living
room, speaking into his radio. After a series of "yups," he
faced Ashton.

"Time to move." He gave a quick smile, revealing a dimple
in his right cheek. "Ready?"

"Where are we going?" Ashton stepped toward the bags
he'd packed after his call to the man in the driveway earlier.
Officer Andrews had urged him to pack, stating that when it
was time to leave, that was it. You were gone.

"We feel it's best to put you in a safe house until we have a
better handle on what sort of threat we're facing."

"A safe house?"

"There's a child involved." He nodded toward the stroller,
where Jaelyn was sleeping soundly.

"And Zoe? Is she coming?"

"A patrol unit will continue to keep an eye on her, and
we've alerted the resort's security team."

"But Morty might try to get to Quentin through me via
her. We dated for a while."

"That's been taken into consideration." The cop gave that dimpled smile again—surely he thought it was disarming, but all it did was frustrate Ashton. "We feel you and the child are at greatest risk right now. We may move Zoe as well, but we try to create as few disturbances in the lives of civilians as we can in situations like this."

"I think she needs protection."

"She has some, and we're analyzing—"

"More."

"We're looking into it," he replied patiently.

Jaelyn began fussing, then outright shrieking until Ashton moved into her line of sight. She stretched her arms to him, her panic palpable.

"I'm here, I'm here," he said, trying to soothe her as he picked her up.

Looking at her, and struck again by how much she'd grown, he realized just how fast life moved on. He'd lost so much in the past few months, but this little child had lost so much more. Her mother, then him, then her birth father. And home after home after home.

She needed stability and love.

He needed stability and love.

"She's got some serious separation anxiety," Officer Andrews commented, as Jaelyn clung to Ashton, her sobs settling. "You said you're her adoptive father?" He'd given Ben the full lowdown on their situation. "Because I'd say she's bonded with you just fine. Is this all you need?" He gestured to Ashton's bags.

"Yes."

"We'll have an escort here in a minute. Things are going to move fast. Just do as we say and trust us." He braced a hand on Ashton's shoulder. "Can you do that?"

"Yes, Officer." He gave a solemn nod. "And thank you."

The man released him and spoke into the radio clipped to his lapel. "Ready to move."

Ashton feared his disappearance would put more of a target on Zoe, and he opened his mouth to say so, but the officer was peeking around the curtain he'd closed upon arrival. He gestured toward the door. Ashton couldn't carry much with Jaelyn clinging to him, so he took the largest bag he could. Several officers came through the door, their expressions serious as they wordlessly took the stack of belongings before ushering Ashton and the baby out the door to the waiting vehicles.

Ashton quickly installed Jaelyn's car seat, and he looked into her eyes as he buckled her in. She smiled around the pacifier in her mouth, her whole face lighting up as he climbed in beside her.

Forgiveness.

She had forgiven him for leaving her. But it still impacted her, filling her with doubt. Just like Zoe. She'd been afraid of him leaving her again.

And now he was.

He'd shut her out when Morty had arrived, and was about to vanish again for who knew how long.

But he still hadn't changed, had he? He hadn't let her all the way in. He was still holding her at arms reach at times.

Ashton realized that while he'd seen forgiveness in Zoe's eyes, he had never truly forgiven himself. Deep down, he felt as though he didn't deserve a second chance for the way he'd abandoned her, for the way he hadn't found a solution to help everyone.

He had to stop shutting her out.

They moved through the quiet streets of Indigo Bay, collecting curious looks from early morning joggers who knew something was up as soon as they spotted the three cars driving in tandem, one a police cruiser, the others unmarked, but still identifiable due to their present company.

One car peeled off down the street that led toward Zoe's.

"What time is it?" Ashton asked. Shouldn't she be at work by now?

She should be coming with them.

"Please," he said, clinging to the seat in front of him, "whatever you do, protect Zoe."

CHAPTER 9

"I'm sorry. What?" Zoe stared groggily at the large man standing on her front step, trying to make sense of his words. She'd come home from her walk on the beach with her mom and had changed into her pj's, then crashed on her bed to think. She'd fallen asleep for what felt like hours, but her clock said it was only a little after nine in the morning.

"We believe your life is in danger, and we need to move you to a safe house."

"A safe house." Zoe seriously needed some coffee to sort this one out. She had crawled out of her cocoon of sleep only because she was worried someone's house was burning down, given the incessant knocking. Well, that and the fact that Logan Stone, Ginger's husband, had phoned her to tell her to answer the door.

"Ashton Wallace mentioned a threat has been made against you."

"How do you know? Who are you?"

The man shifted his weight from foot to foot. He was antsy, that was for certain.

"I'm Zach Forrester."

She blinked at the large man. He was built like a cage fighter and had the scars to back up the image. But there was a gentle confidence to him that put her at ease.

"Logan Stone's associate," he added, his voice as uneven as the cut of his rumpled, dirty blond hair.

"Oh." Zoe rubbed her face. "Why are you here?"

"I hacked into the surveillance at the resort where you work. Morty Gallagher has been keeping tabs on you."

"I think I need to eat something. I don't feel so good."

"We feel it's best to move you somewhere safer until we can neutralize the threat."

Zoe involuntarily took a step back, pressing a hand to her throat.

Neutralize the threat.

Houdini tore past her feet and into the yard. She ran after him, Zach attempting to snag both of them on the way by, and failing. The stones of the walkway were cold under her bare feet, the cat a gray blur as he streaked off.

"Ms. Ward!" Zach called.

"I need to catch him!" Houdini ran into the street, where a black SUV screeched to a halt to avoid the collision.

Grateful, Zoe met the driver's eye as she reached the curb, then jumped back. It was Morty Gallagher, and he was getting out of his vehicle.

* * *

Hours ago, when Ashton and Jaelyn had been placed in a small airplane, he had asked where they were going and where Zoe was. He hadn't received an answer. As the plane landed in what seemed to be the middle of a hot and dry nowhere, he was still clueless.

Back in Indigo Bay, the officers had picked up the pace shortly after one of the vehicles had peeled off toward Zoe's.

Everything had ticked faster then, the officers wordlessly zipping things into place. Ashton and Jaelyn had been shuffled out of town, taken to a private airport and sent on their way.

Ashton climbed down the plane's narrow steps, his stomach growling, the sun high in the sky and Jaelyn asleep on his shoulder. Low rolling hills surrounded the tiny airport. Private hangers lined the single strip of asphalt that served as a runway, with a gravel road running parallel. At the end of the runway he was pretty sure he spied barbed-wire fencing and a herd of cattle grazing in the scruffy underbrush.

"Where are we?" he asked a man who looked like a typical small-town sheriff, all hat, friendly smile and bit of a gut, no doubt thanks to some hearty home-cooked meals.

"Texas," he replied simply. "You're staying in a safe house." The pilot had climbed out of the plane and was loading Ashton's belongings into the back of a pickup truck that was likely as old as the cracked and heaved tarmac beneath his feet.

"How long?"

"Reckon nobody knows. Hours? Weeks? Time'll tell."

The sheriff began pushing him toward the pickup, where a woman in a cowboy hat was waiting. Ashton shifted the child in his arms and placed a hand on the man's shoulder, stopping him. "Where's Zoe Ward? Is she okay?"

"I heard there was a complication back in Indigo Bay, and that private agencies are now involved." He avoided making eye contact. "The less you know, the safer you'll be."

"What? No. No, don't tell me that."

"I'll let you know more when I'm authorized to do so."

Ashton felt the world sway. He had a hollow feeling in his gut that refused to go away. Numbly, he climbed into the truck and, once seated, closed his eyes for a moment, pulling himself together. He would never forgive himself if anything happened to Zoe.

The woman at the wheel reached across Jaelyn's car seat, which had already been installed on the regular cab's one bench seat, her hand outstretched. "Alexa McTavish. Pleased to meet you. Gonna buckle up that little one?"

Ashton snapped out of his daze and settled Jaelyn for the trip.

"Are you an officer?" he asked the woman.

"Nah, I just know some people out in Indigo Bay; and with my rifle skills and new ranch out in the middle of nowhere, they figured I could keep someone safe." She winked as she pulled out of the grassy parking lot.

Ashton looked behind and saw the sheriff following them.

"Don't worry," Alexa said, "there will be twenty-four-hour police surveillance."

"Is this a real safe house? Like you see in the movies?"

"I don't know what kind of movies you watch, but I'm guessing no. But we'll keep you safe."

Ashton supposed that was about all he could ask for at the moment.

* * *

ZOE BLINKED from her spot on the pavement, her head throbbing from a surprise hit. It was cold beneath her, the asphalt under her palms surprisingly gritty. She could see Houdini hiding under a bush across the street, his eyes catching the morning light and his tail twitching.

To her right was Morty, flat out on his back, blinking slowly. His SUV door was still open, the engine running, and Zoe struggled to piece together the flurry of activity that had happened after she'd run into the street. She hadn't been hit by the car, but rather had been clobbered by Morty as he'd tried to abduct her.

Beside her, Zach pounced on the stunned thug, flipping him over as though he weighed nothing, placing his knee squarely on the man's lower back, then whipping his hands behind him and cuffing them.

Several thin wires were strung across the pavement, and Zoe realized Zach had Tased Morty with darts from his spot several feet away.

Thank goodness for Logan's associates. Namely, Zach Forrester. Especially since from nearly half a block away she could see Indigo Bay's most annoying officer, Paul Moore, hoofing it toward them. His so-called surveillance had been a little too discreet, putting him far from the action and definitely too late to play a part in her rescue.

Zoe groaned as she picked herself off the street. Her knees and hands were aching with road rash, and the back of her head was screaming.

If Zach had Morty, did that mean the danger Ashton thought she was in had ended? And what about Ashton?

Zoe's neighbors, Bob and Mary, came rushing out of their home. "Are you okay?" Bob called.

"Stay back!" Zach yelled, hand extended in the classic Stop! position.

Paul had run back for his car, an unmarked sedan, and now he parked it, angled across the street, with a squeal. The light on its dash flashed red and blue, and he jumped out, gun drawn.

"Check the vehicle for more people," Zach commanded.

"Who are you?" shouted Moore.

"Paul, just do it," Zoe snapped. She'd known him since they were kids, and was still surprised he'd not only passed the rigorous training, but had been hired to keep the town safe. He had a thing for procedures, rules and regulations, which sometimes prevented him from doing what was needed—such as watching her house from a close enough distance to be useful.

Paul quickly complied, finding the vehicle empty.

Zach placed Morty in the back of the unmarked police car as if he owned it, making Paul squirm and fidget as though trying to sort out how to jump in and be useful. Zoe watched as Zach and he had words, with Paul just about saluting him at the end.

Zach came over to where Zoe was sitting on the curb, gingerly plucking bits of sand and gravel out of her scraped knees. He helped her up with a surprising tenderness for a man of his size.

"Are you okay?" he asked.

She nodded. "I think so."

"Let's see." He tipped Zoe's head down to check it. "You're going to need stitches."

She touched the back of her head, surprised to find it wet.

Zach waved to the officer, making gestures Zoe didn't understand. Seconds later Paul pulled away, with Morty in his custody.

"What about Ashton?" Zoe asked. "Can someone check on him? Morty was looking for him."

"He's in safe hands."

Zoe was weakened by the relief that rushed through her.

"Let's get you taken care of."

"I have to get my cat first." Zoe looked up, hoping to find Houdini still in the bushes. Instead she found Mary, her neighbor, holding the escapee, eyes wide.

"I've got him, Zoe," she said, her voice higher pitched than usual.

"Can you watch him and the rest of the gang for…" She looked to Zach for an answer on how long she might be gone.

"However long is needed?" he asked firmly, on her behalf.

"Of course, of course." Mary hurried across the street in her slippers and bathrobe, heading toward Zoe's house, where the door was still wide open, the cats scattered through the yard, taking advantage of their freedom.

Zoe thought of all that could have happened during the past five minutes, and turned to the nearest shrub to empty her stomach.

CHAPTER 10

D r. Browning stood under the fluorescent lights in the Indigo Bay police station and stitched up the laceration on the back of Zoe's head, where she'd been struck by Morty. He'd been called in as the officers didn't want her out in public—even with them at her side—if it could be helped. And with it being a small town, the doctor was more than happy to make a house call.

"All fixed up," he declared, as he removed the gloves he'd been wearing. "The stitches will dissolve on their own, so no need to come in and have them removed."

"Can she fly?" Zach asked. He was standing by the door of the interrogation room, arms crossed. He'd been asking the doctor more questions than Officer Tara Powell, making Zoe curious about who was in charge. If Zach didn't have jurisdiction here he was certainly acting as though he did.

"Fly?" Zoe repeated.

"Yes," Dr. Browning told Zach. "Luckily, it's only a minor concussion." He smiled warmly at Zoe. "You may feel your symptoms a little more acutely, is all. Take good care of yourself."

"I will. Thanks."

The man picked up his doctor's bag and exited the room.

"Thanks for coming in," Tara said, seeing him out. She turned to Zach. "You're cleared to take Zoe to the safe house."

"But isn't the danger over?" Zoe asked. "You have Morty in custody."

Zach checked the clip on his gun, a move Zoe found intimidating. He caught her look, but said nothing.

"Men like Morty don't work alone," Tara explained. "Just because we've waylaid him doesn't mean the danger has passed."

Zach added, "Sometimes it means quite the opposite."

Zoe shivered.

"You cold?"

She nodded. Cold, and scared out of her mind. Her only solace was that Ashton was tucked away somewhere safe.

"I'll find you some clothes," Tara said.

Zoe looked down at what she was wearing. Her pajama T-shirt and shorts.

"Will I see Ashton?"

The officer smiled before she slipped from the room. "We'll see." But the way she lifted her eyebrows told Zoe all she needed to know. She was going wherever he was.

* * *

ZOE'S bashed head felt thick with travel and fatigue as the sheriff dropped her off at the Blueberry Creek Ranch II, which she'd guess was located smack-dab in the middle of nowhere. Zach had been sitting silently in the back seat of the cruiser like a shadow, hulking and ever-present.

The sheriff, Conroy Johnson, had filled them in on things on the drive over. Everything from the ranch where she'd be staying, to the people who lived in the remote farmhouses that dotted the land they'd traversed on their way from the basic airstrip she and Zach had landed.

"You'll fit right in. Ashton and his baby are already here."

"What?" *Baby?*

Her heart thrummed with the implications of what that one little word "baby" might imply.

"Ashton and his daughter arrived a few hours back. Cutest little thing. Doesn't want to be parted from her papa."

Papa.

"Is it Jaelyn?" Zoe's heart was pounding so hard now she was surprised the sheriff hadn't heard it and hadn't swung the car around to get her checked out at the nearest medical facility.

"Yep. A good cowgirl name." He grinned as he got out of the car, then hitched his pants as he walked around to the bumper.

Jaelyn. Ashton. They were both here. What had gone on last night while Zoe was trying to sleep?

"You all right?" Zach asked, opening her door.

Zoe nodded, adjusting her borrowed sundress, still not fully processing the news. It didn't matter what avenue her mind went down, she couldn't quite figure out the conclusion. In front of her, an old ranch house sprawled across the green grass. Corrals, horses and barns surrounded the place, with pickup trucks everywhere. It felt like a real Texas ranch, not a safe house.

Zach placed a hand on her elbow, supporting her as he steered her toward the entrance. "I'll be sticking around for a few days, so if anything weird happens, just let me know."

She nodded, ill at ease with the idea of having a bodyguard—of *needing* one.

They climbed the steps to the massive veranda that

wrapped the front of the house, but as the sheriff let himself in, Zoe heard someone say her name from behind.

She turned, and spotted Ashton. There was a small girl propped up in a little red wagon he was pulling, and the look of relief on Ashton's face matched the relief in Zoe's heart. She flew down the steps and into his waiting arms, squeezing him so tight she thought her heart would burst.

"You're okay," he murmured, brushing the hair from her face. "You're okay."

Zoe sniffed back tears. They held each other for a long time before Ashton finally released his tight grip, but still keeping her in a loose embrace.

"I'm so sorry," she said as he placed a firm kiss to her temple. She turned her face so his next kiss landed hard on her lips.

Conroy walked past, announcing, "I'll take my leave now. You're in safe hands here."

Zoe nodded, her focus entirely on Ashton and the concern and love she saw shine for her in his hazel eyes.

"There's nothing to be sorry for," he told her. "I'm the one who's sorry." His hand hovered near her head, his eyes a well of concern. "Are you okay? I heard about Morty."

"I'm okay. It's just a bump." She glanced around for Zach, who was no doubt skulking about the place, taking in bodyguard-type intel.

Zoe gestured to the cute baby with the gorgeous brown skin sitting in the wagon beside Ashton. She'd soon be a toddler, up and walking and talking. "Is this Jaelyn?"

"It is."

Her heart buoyed for Ashton.

"What happened?"

"Quentin passed guardianship to me last night. My name is still on her birth certificate."

"Is that something permanent?" Zoe asked nervously. If

Quentin returned for Jaelyn, she had a feeling it would destroy Ashton. "I'm confused."

"Come inside and I'll explain."

A woman came out the screen door, carrying a tray with a pitcher and two glasses.

"Hi, Zoe. Glad you made it."

"Alexa?" How many people from her life were hiding out? "Is everything okay? I mean, I thought you were still working for Cohen's in Charleston?"

"Welcome to my ranch," the woman said with a smile.

"I thought your ranch was in Montana." Sheriff Johnson had mentioned she'd be staying at Alexa's ranch, but Zoe hadn't clued in that it was the Alexa she knew from back home.

"My sister decided to take it over, so Cash and I moved out here a few months ago, splitting our time between the two places." She set down the drinks near a porch swing. "I'll let you and Ashton catch up on things, then you and I can catch up later, and go over the safe house rules. There's a room made up for you." She headed back inside, and Zach rounded the porch steps to go join her.

Despite the warmth of the day, Zoe shivered.

Safe house. Hiding out. Bodyguard.

Ashton picked up the baby and the diaper bag she'd been settled against, and stepped up onto the porch. He took a seat on the swing, making the girl smile as he set her on his lap. She leaned against him, obviously content.

Zoe followed them, sitting nervously on the edge of the swing.

"I'm sorry I put you in danger," Ashton said. His eyes were dark, as if he hadn't had a thing but worry for company since she'd last seen him.

"You didn't know," she whispered. Her fingers drifted to

the bump on her head. "They caught Morty, but they still think things are still unsecure."

"I heard."

"They have to make sure everything's safe before we return." She felt like she was stating the obvious, but didn't know what else to say. All she wanted to do was curl up in Ashton's arms and never leave.

It was warm, the afternoon sun beating down, but the large trees planted out front shaded the porch.

As Ashton gave Jaelyn big smiles, which were returned full force, he explained how Quentin had practically dumped the girl, while saying he had to stay low for a while.

"Stay low?"

Ashton nodded, explaining how he was fairly confident the man was going to do something illegal to pay Morty money he owed for double-crossing him in what he presumed was a drug-related deal. Why he'd believed he'd never get caught was another question. But until Quentin either paid his debt or the police found him and took matters into their own hands, Ashton, Jaelyn and Zoe were still considered to be at risk.

"You have to make sure he never gets her back. Ever again," Zoe said, gesturing to the child.

"I will." Ashton let Jaelyn slide down his leg and onto her feet. He held her hands while she made gurgling noises and bounced in time to a Travis Tritt song coming through an open window.

"How many of Morty's men do you think are still looking for Quentin?" Zoe asked, glancing at the child, knowing she was too young to comprehend their conversation.

"No clue."

They were silent for a long time.

Then Zoe, watching Jaelyn, who only had eyes for Ashton, stated, "She likes you."

"I was her father for months." He adjusted the girl's sun hat, swallowing over a lump of affection that had clearly blocked his throat. Watching him with Jaelyn made Zoe's heart grow. This was the man she'd fallen in love with last summer, and he was quite possibly even better than he'd been then.

"She's going to have an amazing father who will raise her right," Zoe said, feeling choked up as well. She wanted to complete their family picture—she wanted to be the wife, the mother, and not just a friend or ex-girlfriend.

They sat in silence for a few minutes, the quiet punctuated by the odd refrain drifting from the kitchen or the odd whinny from a horse.

Ashton turned to her, his expression serious. "I'm sorry if you've felt shut out. I was trying to protect you, but protecting you should have meant sharing with you."

"I understand it's difficult to share everything when you haven't known someone for a long time."

He gave her a grateful look. "Still, you deserved to be told what was going on. I know you were scared I was going to leave you, like your ex-fiancé did. And then I disappeared. And when I returned I wasn't as forthcoming as I could have been. And then I shoved you out of my cottage, too."

"The old stuff shouldn't matter," Zoe said hesitantly. "And I know you were trying to protect me."

"It does matter. It's a part of who we are."

Jaelyn had sat down on the porch floor and was reaching for a cat that had come by, rubbing against her and making her squeal. She tried to put her mouth on the cat, but Ashton was there, directing her away.

"But I also understand that sometimes, when we're so overwhelmed by something, we're afraid if we talk about it we might break," Zoe said quietly, thinking of all he'd been through. "When Kurtis broke up with me the night before our wedding, my mom saw my expression and demanded to know what was going on. I only managed to shake my head before fleeing to my hotel room to have a breakdown."

Jaelyn patted Ashton and said, "Ba-ba." He lifted her onto his lap, settling her as he expertly pulled a ready bottle out of the diaper bag. Jaelyn plucked it from his grasp and started chugging the contents.

"So I think I understand how you felt," Zoe said. It was still awful to think that he had been feeling that way, though, and hadn't been able to talk to her. "And I'm sorry you couldn't speak about it."

"It's not your fault."

"Sometimes I'm too…"

"You're perfect," Ashton said, firmly and kindly. "It was me. Don't blame yourself."

"But if I had been—"

"No. There's nothing in your actions in need of forgiving. I should have listened to my gut. If I had, it would've told me that if I couldn't talk to you about it, and that if I feared you'd talk me out of it, then I was doing the wrong thing."

"How was it the wrong thing?" she asked gently. "Jaelyn needed a father and you were there for her. What would have happened to her if you hadn't been?"

* * *

ASHTON BLINKED AT ZOE, wondering indeed what would have happened to Jaelyn if he hadn't stepped up. It likely wouldn't have been good.

"I'm glad you were there for her," Zoe said. She smiled at the child in Ashton's lap, and Jaelyn threw her empty bottle onto the porch and reached for Zoe.

Zoe's eyes lit up as Ashton transferred the baby into her arms. They looked so natural together that he felt a flash of guilt for wanting this. Someone else's child. Their lives in such disrepair so he could have *this*. Something wonderful. A blessing borne from someone else's dysfunction and tragedy.

It felt natural having Jaelyn back in his life, and it felt just as right sharing her with Zoe. He hoped it would be forever.

"Maliki knew Jaelyn wasn't mine, but she needed someone…" He let out a long, slow breath, resolved to tell Zoe every detail whether she wanted to know them or not. "She needed someone to raise her after she was gone. She chose the baby's life over her own when she passed up treatment and medication that would have kept her healthy in order for Jaelyn to be born without…without more issues." He looked at the precious child, his heart breaking for the choice her mother had had to make.

"Oh, Ash."

"Because of it, she died before her time."

Zoe had closed her eyes, clearly feeling his pain. She was so empathetic… Why had he ever convinced himself that she would judge him harshly for stepping in and helping them?

"She was lucky to have you there," Zoe said.

But it had meant excluding Zoe from his heart and dreams.

"Maliki didn't have a family, growing up, and she wanted Jaelyn to have what she didn't." He shook his head. "She was sacrificing so much, giving up her own health for the baby's, and I wanted to do right by her." He studied his hands. "I'm sorry I hurt you."

"It was an impossible choice."

"I was afraid if I talked to you that I wouldn't put their health first, and I knew I had to even though it meant losing what I really wanted. I thought she was my child, and I didn't want to be a deadbeat dad."

"You'd never be like your father."

"You don't know how tempting it was, Zoe. To choose love over obligation. What I wanted over what they needed."

Zoe sighed as they both looked at the child that wasn't theirs. Jaelyn let out a shriek and stretched for the floor.

"You were used," Zoe said simply, putting Jaelyn down so she could crawl again.

Ashton bowed his head, shame washing over him. To his surprise, he felt arms snake their way around his torso, making the swing rock. Zoe. She hugged him tightly.

"I can't even imagine what turmoil and emotion you've been through over the past year."

"Can you forgive me?"

"There's nothing to forgive. You tried your best and are a good man. The very best kind."

He hugged Zoe back, promising himself he'd never let her go, never take a day for granted ever again.

CHAPTER 11

A shton balanced Jaelyn on his hip. She was getting sleepy and he moved her up so she could rest on his chest, using his shoulder for a pillow as he waited for Zoe to be done on the phone in the lobby of the Indigo Bay Cottages.

It had been a week and a half since their return, after spending three days in Alexa's safe house. It turned out that Quentin had taken a pile of cocaine from Morty, promising to sell it. Well, he had, but then he'd spent the cash instead of passing it on to Morty. The police were able to sort out the issue within a few days, piling charges upon charges on both men as they dug deeper and deeper into the recent deal.

Zach Forrester had returned to Indigo Bay with the three of them to keep an eye on things for a while. And before he'd declared all to be well, he'd installed security systems at both Zoe's house and the apartment Ashton was now renting for himself and Jaelyn. Then, just as suddenly as he'd arrived in Zoe's life, Zach had vanished—but not before melting little Jaelyn's heart. Zach had been the first name she'd learned to say.

Ashton swayed with Jaelyn in his arms and she grew heavy as sleep pulled at her.

"Well, I don't know, Moe," Zoe was saying into the phone. "It doesn't sound like the kind of marriage situation where she's looking to have a honeymoon."

Ashton frowned. That seemed like a strange thing to say.

"I understand. Well, maybe call it a little getaway. Does Amy enjoy the ocean? We've got..."

She listened in that patient way of hers, no doubt determined to find the right vacation for the two soon-to-be-marrieds.

She caught sight of Ashton and Jaelyn, her face lighting up. She held up a finger, asking him to wait for her to finish her call.

"Uh-huh. Yep," she said quickly. "I'll book the cottage for two days at the end of August, then. You can cancel a week before your arrival for a full refund. Although since you're a cousin of Dallas's I'm sure he'd be happy to allow you to cancel right up until the last minute." She smiled, listening again. "Okay. Good luck with your wedding." She added quickly, "And thank Ginger and Logan for me."

Zoe shivered as she ended the call, and Ashton had no doubt that the thank-you she'd asked Moe to pass along to his friend Ginger wasn't for the resort referral, but for the way her husband had sent Zach her way—and in the knick of time, from her retelling of the story. Ashton sure hadn't liked hearing about how Morty had almost abducted her, and he had a feeling both he and Zoe would be having some bad dreams for quite a few nights to come.

Ashton stepped up to Zoe's desk. "That sounded like an odd conversation."

"Give me a sec. He said I can add him to the newsletter list." She began typing, and over her shoulder Ashton saw her work the newsletter program like a ninja. She had gotten the hang of it, that was for certain.

"He's one of Ginger's friends from Blueberry Springs," she said as she typed, "and he's marrying his best friend, who's just turned thirty. Long story…" Zoe looked up as she finished her task. "I need to give that woman a referral discount next time she comes."

Zoe stood and came around the desk. She hugged Ashton, her embrace including the child in his arms who reached out to pat Zoe's cheek, making them both smile. "I'm so glad things can go back to normal again for us all."

"Me, too."

"I did some thinking in Texas."

"Yeah? What's that?" Ashton loved the way a sunbeam filtering through a skylight was giving his Zoe a beautiful glow. Their new rhythm as a couple, as the adults in Jaelyn's life felt right. More right than he'd ever been able to imagine, and he hoped that soon Zoe would be ready to take the next step in their relationship.

"I'm done moving slowly," she announced, surprising Ashton. "I'm done needing to know every gritty little thing in your life."

"What?"

"Ash, your daughter needs a mother."

He nodded slowly. He had a feeling he knew what was coming, but hesitated to allow his imagination to head off that way.

"I would like to be that person for her, and I would also like to be your loving wife. Will you and your daughter marry me?"

Ashton's heart felt two sizes too big for his chest all of a sudden, and as though it was going to burst from overflowing with love. And it was the most wonderful feeling in the world.

"I love you, Zoe." He shifted Jaelyn so he could cup Zoe's face with his free hand, giving her a sweet kiss that wouldn't be the last one of the day, week, or year. It was just the beginning of many.

"I love you, too."

"I thought we were going to try moving slowly? Build up a foundation of trust and sharing?"

"Moving slow is for chumps. I vote we put a ring on this finger." She wiggled her ring-free left hand in front of them, causing him to laugh. It felt good. Whatever walls they'd erected after the breakup were long gone now, and it was like old times, only better.

"Okay," he said. "Let's get engaged."

"Done."

"Done?"

"Yes. And I happen to know someone who does wedding ceremony coordinating here at Indigo Bay Cottages, and there's an opening this weekend."

Ashton nearly choked. "You're serious?"

Jaelyn had resisted sleep and was patting his cheek, gurgling softly to herself. She gave a happy little squeal and reached for Zoe, who took her without a second thought, bouncing the girl on her hip.

Ashton loved that Zoe was moving so quickly, but he was worried, too. "I thought you were afraid to move fast this time?" he asked carefully.

"I was scared."

"And?"

"We've been through a lot. I love you. You love me. That fact still remains, and I happen to think it's the most important one of all."

She gave him a moment to absorb her logic.

"And," she added with a twinkle in her eye, "if you're

married to me it's harder for you to run away and marry someone else."

He tipped his head back and let out a bark of laughter, making Jaelyn jump in Zoe's arms.

"Zoe Ward, I would be honored to be your first and last husband."

"Last husband?" she teased as Dallas approached.

"Definitely."

"I know a guy who can get you a ring," Dallas said, leaning against Zoe's desk. "What? I saw what was happening here. You're engaged, but you need rings. Congratulations, by the way."

"We'll need two rings," Ashton said to Dallas. "By Friday."

"Three," Zoe said decisively. "I think Jaelyn should have some sort of family ring for when she'd older that will show she's a part of us." She said to Ashton, "It's not just the two of us entering a marriage, we're creating a family."

"So not wedding bands, but family rings?" Ashton clarified.

"Exactly." She pulled him closer to give him a kiss. "I knew there was a reason I chose you. We like to hang out on the same wavelength."

EPILOGUE

Zoe smiled at Ashton, who was waiting for her on the sunny beach. His dark cummerbund and bow tie brought out the somberness of his hazel eyes, and she wondered how she'd ever been so lucky as to have a second chance with the man of her dreams.

He was holding Jaelyn in his arms and she was so adorable in her fluffy dress it brought tears to Zoe's eyes.

Family. Despite the pain of the past year, she was going to wind up right where she'd hoped she would be.

Her bare feet flew across the sand as she launched herself at Ashton and Jaelyn. Her parents laughed and cheered, as did her special out-of-town guests, Ginger and Logan, as well as Logan's associate, Zach.

Ashton and Jaelyn laughed as Zoe danced around them, giving them each a quick kiss.

"Let's get married!"

Dallas, the master of ceremonies, rolled his eyes good-naturedly at Zoe, looking totally pleased for her. The man was single, but one day he'd find The One, and he'd no longer be rolling his eyes, she knew. He'd be right there in the thick of it. The wonderful, wonderful thick of it.

Jaelyn was handed off to Ashton's best man, but immediately reached back for her father. He said quickly to Dallas, "You'd better hurry, before she blows."

The poor child had separation issues that were going to be tough to deal with when Ashton began work in August, leaving her with a sitter they'd not yet chosen. But Dr. Browning had said Jaelyn's anxiety was normal, and that she'd soon acclimatize to having a stable family. It would just take time.

Dallas zipped through their vows, and they exchanged simple wedding bands, which the local jeweler had created for them, ensuring Jaelyn got one, too, for when she was old enough to wear one.

When Dallas told the newlyweds that they could seal the deal with a kiss, Zoe slipped into Ashton's waiting arms, her right hand stroking the short, smooth hair at the base of his neck. He felt like everything she had ever wanted. They kissed.

"I now announce you husband and wife!" Dallas called out.

Ashton kissed Zoe again.

"I like being married," she told him.

Ashton laughed. "So far, so good."

Zoe prepared to toss her bouquet, not wanting to wait until later. She launched the flowers in an arc high above her, the ribbons trailing through the picture-perfect blue sky.

She turned to see who had caught them and laughed. It was a very surprised looking Zach. His beefy hands seemed out of place clutching the delicate flowers, but he smiled good-naturedly.

He asked, "Can you order a wife online? Because that's the only way I'm ever going to find someone to marry me."

"That's not how it works," Ginger said, patting his arm. "But don't worry, we'll find you someone before you resort to online shopping for the love of your life. Right, Zoe?"

Zoe turned to Ashton. "I think Ginger can definitely be trusted for finding one's soul mate."

* * *

Six fun beach reads by Six fabulous authors

Have you read them all?

Sweet Dreams (Book 1) by Stacy Claflin

Sweet Matchmaker (Book 2) by Jean Oram

Sweet Sunrise (Book 3) by Kay Correll

Sweet Illusions (Book 4) by Jeanette Lewis

Sweet Regrets (Book 5) by Jennifer Peel

Sweet Rendezvous (Book 6) by Danielle Stewart

Sweet Saturdays (Book 7) by Pamela Kelley

Sweet Beginnings (Book 8) by Melissa McClone

Sweet Starlight (Book 9) by Kay Correll

Sweet Forgiveness (Book 10) by Jean Oram

Sweet Reunion (Book 11) by Stacy Claflin

Sweet Entanglement (Book 12) by Jean C. Gordon

More coming in 2019!

Note: This series can be read out of order.

MORE INDIGO BAY

Get swept away for the holidays! Come visit Indigo Bay at Christmas with our holiday short stories.

Holiday Short Stories

Sweet Holiday Surprise by Jean Oram

Sweet Holiday Memories by Kay Correll

Sweet Holiday Wishes by Melissa McClone

Sweet Holiday Traditions by Danielle Stewart

HAVE YOU BEEN TO BLUEBERRY SPRINGS?

Fun, sweet romances that will warm your heart and make you laugh out loud.

Read, Dream, Laugh & Love
Sweet, Laugh-out-Loud, Feel-Good Reads

Book 1: Whiskey and Gumdrops (Mandy & Frankie)

Book 2: Rum and Raindrops (Jen & Rob)

Book 3: Eggnog and Candy Canes (Katie & Nash)

Book 4: Sweet Treats (3 short stories—Mandy, Amber, & Nicola)

Book 5: Vodka and Chocolate Drops (Amber & Scott)

Book 6: Tequila and Candy Drops (Nicola & Todd)

Companion Novel: Champagne and Lemon Drops (Beth & Oz)

THERE'S EVEN MORE INDIGO BAY IN
BLUEBERRY SPRINGS WITH THE VEILS
AND VOWS SERIES!

Continue the adventure with irresistible, humorous feel-good
reads you've come to count on from Jean Oram. Keep flipping
the pages all through the night with the Veils and Vows series.

IRRESISTIBLE & ADDICTIVE
THE LATEST FROM BLUEBERRY SPRINGS...

The Promise (Book 0: Devon & Olivia)

The Surprise Wedding (Book 1: Devon & Olivia)

A Pinch of Commitment (Book 2: Ethan & Lily)

The Wedding Plan (Book 3: Luke & Emma)

Accidentally Married (Book 4: Burke & Jill)

The Marriage Pledge (Book 5: Moe & Amy)

Mail Order Soulmate (Book 6: Zach & Catherine)

Companion stories set in Indigo Bay series:

Sweet Matchmaker (Ginger and Logan)

Sweet Holiday Surprise (Alexa and Cash)

Sweet Forgiveness (Zoe and Ashton)

THE SUMMER SISTERS

Come get swept away...

TAMING BILLIONAIRES HAS NEVER BEEN SO SWEET
Now in Audio

Love and Rumors

Love and Dreams

Love and Trust

Love and Danger

Love and Mistletoe

ABOUT JEAN ORAM

Jean Oram is a *New York Times* and *USA Today* bestselling romance author who loves making opposites attract in tear-jerking, feel-good, sweet romances set in small towns. She grew up in a town of 100 (cats and dogs not included) and owns one pair of high heels which she has worn approximately three times in the past twenty years. Jean lives near a lake in Canada with her husband, two kids, cat, dog and those pesky deer who keep wandering into her yard to eat her rose bushes and apple trees.

Become an Official Fan: www.facebook.com/groups/jeanoramfans

Newsletter: www.jeanoram.com/signup

Twitter: www.twitter.com/jeanoram

Facebook: www.facebook.com/JeanOramAuthor

Instagram: www.instagram.com/Author_JeanOram

Website & blog: www.jeanoram.com